How badly [obscured by barcode] trust?

A soft knock sounded on the door, and Abner pulled it open. The pizza delivery.

"Did you want some?" His throat tightened. The last time they'd had pizza together had been their date before the TV disaster that broke them up.

Although he respected her new beliefs, he missed the old Rebecca. Did she still have fun?

"Remember when—" he started to say, but she shook her head. "Look, Rebecca, we have a past together."

"A past I'd rather forget."

The lump in his throat was so huge he could barely swallow. "We can't eliminate the past, and I hope we can't erase the love we had—still have—for each other. I understand you can't trust me anymore, but can't we enjoy those memories?"

"We don't agree on our goals for the future, so it's easier to leave all that behind and move forward with our separate lives."

Separate goals. Separate lives. Separate futures.

But all he wanted was to be together...

A former teacher and librarian, **Rachel J. Good** is the author of more than 2,300 articles and forty books in print or forthcoming under several pseudonyms. She grew up near Lancaster County, Pennsylvania, the setting for her Amish novels. Striving to be as authentic as possible, she spends time with her Amish friends, doing chores on their farm and attending family events. Rachel loves to travel and visit many different Amish communities. Rachel enjoys meeting readers and speaks regularly at book events, schools, libraries, churches, book clubs and conferences across the country. Find out more about her at www.racheljgood.com.

BIG CITY AMISH

Rachel J. Good

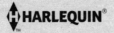

Recycling programs
for this product may
not exist in your area.

ISBN-13: 978-1-335-45495-9

Big City Amish

This edition published by arrangement with Harlequin Books S.A.

For questions and comments about the quality of this book,
please contact us at CustomerService@Harlequin.com.

Printed in U.S.A.

Chapter One

December gusts rattled the windows as Rebecca Zook sliced freshly baked homemade bread for sandwiches. The coal stove in the basement warmed the kitchen, but outside, brisk winds whipped newly fallen snow into swirling eddies that pattered the windows with tiny pellets of ice. Bare branches of maples scratched against the window, and Rebecca shivered.

Grateful she'd finished her Saturday morning chores, she buttered the bread and spread mustard on the opposite side before layering the slices with American cheese and Lebanon bologna. She cut each sandwich into neat triangles and added a red beet egg, potato chips, and broccoli slaw to each plate.

A loud banging on the front door startled her, and she jumped. Who was calling on a Saturday morning? From time to time, people stopped by to ask *Dat*'s advice. Because he'd been the former bishop, many in their community relied on his wisdom and insight. She hurried to the door, but when she turned the knob and pulled it open, she skidded to a stop.

"Abner?" Frigid winds blew through the door, chilling her body, matching the iciness inside her heart. Rebecca lowered her gaze to avoid meeting his eyes. One glance into those sparkling brown eyes, and she'd be lost, drowning in their magnetic pull. "I'm not allowed to—" Her parents had forbidden her to see him unless they were chaperoned, but that was no longer an issue. She'd broken up with him after she'd discovered...

Her older brother, Jakob, rushed up the sidewalk behind him. "Hello, Abner. Come on in." He motioned for Rebecca to open the door wider.

What was going on with Jakob? Why was he being so friendly? While she'd dated Abner, Jakob had followed them around and begged her to break up with his one-time best friend. Now he was inviting him in for a visit?

"Come on," Jakob insisted. "It's freezing out here."

Reluctantly, Rebecca opened the door, but Abner shifted on the doorstep as if he wished to flee. With a pleading glance at her, he flicked his head in the direction of the car he'd parked in the driveway. "I just need to speak with you for a few minutes." His husky voice brought back memories best forgotten. "Alone, please?"

Before Rebecca could answer, Jakob snapped, "Absolutely not."

Rebecca clenched her fists at her side. She could issue her own denial. She didn't need Jakob interfering in her relationship. A relationship that had ended. Though she'd been about to say *no*, she changed her mind. "I'll get my coat."

Relief washed over Abner's face, but a storm cloud crossed her brother's. "You're not supposed to—"

Holding up a hand to stop his warning, she threw

Jakob a pleading glance. "Abner needs to talk. I'll be sitting in his car in plain sight. You can even stand at the window to watch us."

She slipped her arms into the sleeves of her black wool coat, tied on her black bonnet, and stepped onto the porch. Her foot hit an icy patch, and she skidded along the painted wooden floorboards. Arms flailing, she grabbed the porch railing and managed to stay upright. Abner reached for her arm, but she sidled away, and he dropped his hand to his side.

Rebecca clutched the stair rail as she descended. The last thing she needed was to get within touching distance. Even the slightest brush against his sleeve would be her undoing.

The slats of the living room blind lifted to reveal Jakob standing at the window, glowering. Or maybe not exactly a glower. His forehead was knotted into deep lines of worry. Although she understood her brother's concerns, deep inside, Rebecca still trusted Abner.

He hurried over to open the car door for her. "I was hoping we could drive somewhere private to talk."

Rebecca had already stretched the boundaries beyond what she should. With Jakob staring at them, she shook her head. "I promised my parents…" She let her words trail off. She shouldn't blame this on her family.

Abner was well aware that she made her own decisions. She'd defied her parents when she'd sneaked out to date him. But after the fiasco with the New York producer, she'd come to her own conclusions. Though it had come late, now that she'd turned twenty-one, *Rumschpringa* was officially over for her. She'd committed to starting baptismal classes in the spring, so she could join the church.

Once Abner slid into the car, he turned on the heater. Rebecca could have invited him into the house, where they would have been warmer, but whatever he planned to talk about evidently couldn't be said in front of Jakob.

"You said you had something to tell me?" Instinctively, her body swayed toward him, and Rebecca forced herself to huddle against the car door. Being this close to him stirred too many memories, and she clenched her hands in her lap to still their trembling.

Abner caught the movement, and sadness flickered in his eyes. "I know I don't deserve your friendship or trust, and I don't blame you." He pinched his lips together and tapped his fingers on the steering wheel. After a moment, he said, "I regret acting like a fool, but I never meant to hurt you."

The misery in his voice tore at Rebecca's heart. Her throat too tight to answer, she only nodded. Despite the past, she believed him. But that didn't mean they had a future together. She'd committed to joining the church; he hadn't.

"Do you think we can ever start over?"

The thought was tempting, but she shook her head. "We shouldn't even have been dating when we were not with the church." Rebecca waved a hand at the car's interior. "And judging from this, you aren't ready to give up *Rumschpringa* yet."

"I've needed the car to get to work."

Rebecca narrowed her eyes. "Plenty of people in our community drive buggies or hire *Englisch* drivers."

Abner shifted uneasily. "I thought about that, but hiring cars is expensive."

"You could carpool with some of the other workers. Besides, don't you have to pay for the car and gas?"

"The car is paid for, although I still need to pay for insurance and gas. But all that doesn't matter because I may not have the car much longer."

Rebecca's nose and fingers stung from the cold, but the hope blossoming inside warmed her. "You're ready to join the church?"

"I promised you I would."

Several months ago, Abner had agreed to go to baptismal classes with her in May, but Rebecca worried he only planned to do it to please her. His heart didn't seem to be in it, and he hadn't contacted the bishop yet. Giving up the car must be a sign he was serious about the commitment.

She smiled at him. "You're taking the first steps."

Abner winced and gripped the steering wheel. "It would be easier to let you believe that," he muttered, "but it wouldn't be true."

If only he could reach out and wipe the furrows from her brow, but she'd made it clear earlier his touch wouldn't be welcome. For a moment, after he'd gotten into the car, she'd leaned toward him, and he'd held his breath, hoping…

But she'd quickly drawn away.

And just now when she'd assumed he was giving up the car to join the church, she'd flashed him that adoring smile. The smile that set his pulses racing. The smile that set his world afire. The smile that had gotten him into trouble. Major trouble.

All he wanted to do was reach out, draw her into his arms, and tell her everything would be all right. But he could never erase the past. He'd hurt her—and lost her—by not being completely honest. He'd vowed he'd never do that again. Ever.

A thought flickered briefly through his mind. If he backtracked and said he was giving up the car for the church, would she let him hold her? Maybe agree to start over? He shook his head. No matter what it cost him, he wouldn't lie.

With a sharp pang in his chest, he turned toward her and looked her straight in the eyes. "I have to sell it. I don't have any choice."

Was there some softness behind the question in her eyes? They'd both learned to value honesty. And she knew him so well, perhaps she'd sensed his inner battle.

"I, um, won't have a job soon." The last thing a man should admit to a girl he wanted to marry.

"What did you—" Rebecca snapped her mouth shut. Then she lowered her gaze and murmured, "Sorry." She sighed. "I guess you were expecting that to happen."

"I was, but this isn't because of my behavior. Ever since, you know"—he flapped his hands in the air, praying he wouldn't have to put it into words—"I've been trying to stay out of trouble." And he'd succeeded. Although he'd had to take off quite a few days recently.

Rebecca's eyebrows rose. "Really?"

Did she have to look so surprised? Or was that a flash of disappointment in her eyes? She'd always enjoyed being a rebel.

Abner's lips curved into a smile at the memories. "Yes, I've been a model employee. Even Myron has said so."

"Your boss actually said that?" Rebecca's eyebrows moved so high they almost touched the tight, glossy brown rolls of hair that wound their way around her head from her center part and tucked under her heart-shaped cap.

Abner tore his gaze away and forced himself to answer her question. "He's said it several times."

"Well, that's quite a change."

"Yes, it is." Abner swallowed hard. "Realizing I almost ruined your reputation that night at the barn, well, it changed me."

"Me too," Rebecca admitted.

Abner would give anything to go back to that night. This time he'd shelter and protect her, instead of showing off and shaming them both.

"It's over now, and everything's been fixed." Rebecca exhaled a soft sigh. "Thank God."

"Actually, thanks to Sarah and her grandmother." Abner didn't want to upset Rebecca, but he saw the situation as human intervention, rather than a divine miracle. Although even he had to admit the producer agreeing to destroy the demo had been a miracle. Why had he ever thought it would be a good idea to agree to a screen test? And even worse, why had he involved the woman he loved?

The sideways look Rebecca shot him showed she didn't like his response.

They'd argued about this many times before. He'd explained why he struggled to believe God was in control of every circumstance. If He was, why did He let *Dat* die in a farming accident, leaving behind five children? And what about *Mamm*?

"If you're doing so well at work," Rebecca asked, "why are you worried about losing your job?"

"Myron's son built a *daadi haus* for Myron and his wife, so they're retiring and closing their farmers market stands. He won't need me after next week."

"Oh, Abner, I'm so sorry. I know how hard it was for you to find a job to fit around your *mamm*'s schedule."

"That may not be an issue anymore. That's what I wanted to talk about."

His cell phone chimed, and Rebecca frowned as he pulled it out of his pocket to see who was calling.

A New York number. One he knew by heart. One he had no intention of answering.

Rebecca glanced at the phone, and her frown deepened. She didn't know who it was, did she? He clicked the phone off and jammed it into his pocket.

"Who was that?" The suspicion in her voice told him she'd guessed or at least suspected.

He'd promised himself he wouldn't lie to her ever again, but he couldn't bring himself to say the name. "Someone I never want to speak to again."

"Then why is he calling?"

If she knew enough to say "he," she'd recognized the number. "I have no idea and don't intend to find out." He'd put all that behind him and made a fresh start. A few days ago, he planned to tell Rebecca that, to see if they could do the same. Instead, he'd been hit with devastating news, so today he had something else to say to her, some of the hardest words he'd ever have to say.

He'd been hoping she'd comfort him, but her pinched lips didn't indicate she'd be in a receptive mood.

If God was in control, why had the phone rung just then? Right when he needed Rebecca's support and acceptance most? Why was he losing his job just when *Mamm* needed his income most? And now that he'd given up his chance at stardom, why had the world crashed down around him?

Rebecca's face and toes were icy because the car heater barely warmed the air. It wasn't as cold as a buggy, but she should go—both to warm up and to get away from temptation. The car windows had fogged up, but through the mist, her brother's shadowy figure beckoned to her.

She reached for the door handle. "Jakob's glaring." Her brother's face was too blurred for her to tell, but even without seeing him, she had no doubt her words were true.

"Wait." Abner reached out but stopped before putting a hand on her sleeve.

Rebecca's skin tingled with anticipation. When he returned his hand to the steering wheel, she tamped down her disappointment and desire. But she couldn't stop the small sigh escaping from her lips.

Abner stared at her, his eyes burning with such longing, such hunger, she gripped the door handle to keep herself in place. If he reached out to her now, she'd surrender. Coming out here had been a mistake. "I—I need to go," she croaked out.

"Please stay." His white-knuckled hands gripped the steering wheel. "I haven't told you what I came to say."

The desperation in his voice kept her glued to the car seat, although common sense urged her to flee. But this was Abner, the man she loved with every fiber of her being, and he needed her.

Words rushed from his mouth as if he worried she'd leave before he could finish. "*Mamm*'s been feeling ill for months now. I finally convinced her to see the doctor. He sent her for a bunch of tests and…and"—his voice dropped so low, she could barely hear him—"she has…cancer."

The words hit Rebecca like a gut punch. She doubled over, hugging her arms around her, as if that could ward off the pain. She'd always loved Abner's mother. In fact, over the past few years, she'd confided in Adah more than in her own mother.

Rebecca pulled herself up short. This wasn't about her. Abner had just been dealt two crushing blows. Losing his job and possibly his *mamm* at the same time. She had no idea how he'd deal with all this. Not when his *mamm* had been the center of his life since his *dat*'s death. At fourteen, he'd taken on the care of his four younger brothers, helped support them by taking a job at Miller's Meats in the market, and run the family farm.

With all that pressure, it was no wonder he'd rebelled. At sixteen, he'd bought a car and a cell phone, and she'd starting dating him in secret. They'd both gone a little wild. But Abner had never neglected his siblings or his *mamm*.

"Oh, Abner, no." Her heart cried out for him. Without thinking, she reached out. As soon as her hand touched his sleeve, she knew she'd made a mistake. It might have only been her imagination, but the warmth of his skin, even under his heavy wool coat, penetrated her hand, and her blood zinged.

"Rebecca," he murmured. "I need you, now more than ever."

He bent toward her, and Rebecca tilted her head to meet his lips. She'd comfort him any way she could.

Chapter Two

Inches from her upturned lips, Abner jerked back and pounded the steering wheel with his fist. What was he doing? As much as he wanted to kiss her, he had no right to touch her. Not now. And maybe not ever.

"I'm sorry," he managed to push out past gritted teeth. "I shouldn't have done that."

Rebecca didn't respond, only stared at him with such compassion, he wanted to enfold her in his arms. Most likely, she wouldn't resist. Though he would have welcomed the embrace, he didn't want her pity. He wanted her love.

The front door of the house banged open. Jakob must have seen that almost kiss. Abner had to finish his explanation and leave. Right away.

"The reason I came over today is to deliver a message from *Mamm*. She wondered if you could come to the house to talk with her."

At Rebecca's puzzled frown, he shrugged. "I don't know. She only asked me to deliver the message."

"I could come later this afternoon. Or with tomorrow being an off Sunday, I'd be able to stop by then."

Because church was held every other week, they'd have no services tomorrow. That might be a good time for Rebecca to visit. "*Mamm* usually naps most afternoons, so if you could come before our dinner at twelve thirty, that would be best."

Jakob stepped onto the porch, and Rebecca opened the car door. "I'll do that."

"What time?" Abner pressed. "I'll come to pick you up."

"You don't need to do that." Her forbidding tone made it sound as if she meant to say, *I don't want to ride with you.*

He ignored the hurt. "I insist. A car is better than riding in a buggy in freezing weather." Most cars, that is. The heat in this one barely warmed the air, and their breaths rose in steamy clouds when they spoke, but at least she'd be out of the gusts that threatened to rip the car door from her hands.

"Would eleven work?" She grimaced as the wind whipped at the door again.

Abner managed to temper the enthusiastic response threatening to burst from his lips. "That'll be fine." No, it would be *wunderbar*. Both for him and his *mamm*.

Rebecca hopped out of the car before Jakob marched over and dragged her out. Usually, she appreciated her brother's care and protection, but not today. And not with Abner.

Her brother had been one of the strongest advocates for breaking up with Abner. Jakob had almost convinced their parents to forbid Rebecca to see Abner. She'd defied them all, but sadly, Jakob had turned out to be right.

"I'm coming," she called to her brother in a tear-choked voice. Her heart ached for Abner and for his *mamm*.

Jakob was waiting by the front door when she pulled it open. "Rebecca, I'm worried about you. Sarah confirmed that you broke up with Abner, but after today, I'm finding it hard to believe."

"She's telling the truth." After much prayer, Rebecca had done what she felt God was leading her to do, even though it had broken her heart.

"I have no doubt Sarah's being truthful, but she refuses to repeat any of the conversation she heard that night. She claims only you can divulge what was said."

Rebecca's best friend, Sarah, who was now her brother's fiancée, was the best and most loyal friend anyone could have. "Tell her she has my permission to share anything we said that night."

"You'll need to tell her yourself." Jakob's soppy smile showed his infatuation. "Even though I'm sure she trusts me completely, she'll need your permission."

"You're lucky to be marrying such an exemplary wife." Rebecca meant it as a teasing dig against her brother, who was upright to a fault, but he took her seriously.

"Yes, I am." A sober expression on his face, he gazed off into space. "I only hope I prove worthy."

"You'll do fine," she assured him. "Sarah thinks the world of you."

Jakob frowned. He avoided anything prideful; he took their *dat*'s warnings about *hochmut* to heart. She, on the other hand, craved compliments and attention. If only she were more like Jakob and Sarah. If she were, she and Abner never would have been partying at Yoder's barn that night, and they would have avoided the embarrassing consequences.

Rebecca breathed a sigh of relief, both because that potential scandal had been scuttled and because Jakob had gotten sidetracked from the lecture she suspected he'd been about to deliver. "Dinner is ready." She headed down the hall, with Jakob on her heels. When they reached the kitchen, she handed him two filled plates.

Jakob glanced at the battery-powered clock on the kitchen wall and grimaced. "Only fifteen minutes left to feed *Dat* before I have to head back to work. It often takes him forty-five minutes to eat."

Rebecca wanted to point out he could have been feeding *Dat* instead of spying on her, but she chose the path of peace. "That's my fault, so I can finish feeding him."

"Danke." Jakob took the plates and started from the kitchen. "By the way, what were you and Abner talking about all that time?"

Her younger, sassier, rebellious self would have used the *Englisch* expression, *None of your business*. But Rebecca had spent time on her knees getting right with God before making her decision to join the church. She was striving to lead a godlier life, so she answered his question. "He came to tell me Adah has cancer."

A look of shock crossed Jakob's face. "I'm so sorry to hear that. I'll organize a fundraiser for her."

Her brother often organized fundraisers. They'd done an extremely successful one right after Thanksgiving for a baby's heart operation.

"I'm sure he'd appreciate that." Because Jakob and Abner used to be best friends, she added, "Especially now that he's lost his job at Miller's."

Jakob groaned. "I wonder what Abner did to make Myron issue that ultimatum. Myron's been like a father to him and put up with all his shenanigans."

That was true. Myron had forgiven Abner again and again. But Myron hadn't been a pushover. He'd also lectured Abner and issued consequences that fit each "crime." Though Abner's antics weren't really crimes, he did cross the line when it came to proper Amish behavior. Unlike many of their friends who behaved decorously during *Rumschpringa*, Abner had experimented with *Englisch* life.

This time, though, Abner was innocent, and Rebecca hurried to his defense. "He didn't do anything wrong. Myron's retiring."

"I see." Jakob nodded. "That makes sense. But what will Abner do if he and his mother are both out of work? The family will need some financial help. I'll mention this to Bishop Troyer."

Rebecca cringed inside. Abner and his *mamm* had worked hard from the time his *dat* died to support themselves without help from others. The last thing he'd want is to be a charity case. "I don't know if—"

Jakob cut her off. "I'm well aware of Abner's views on charity, but sometimes you have to accept help."

Would Jakob be willing to accept help? Somehow Rebecca doubted it. But she held her tongue. Fighting with Jakob wouldn't change his mind. If he believed it was the right thing, he wouldn't budge. Besides, once she told him tomorrow's plans, she'd face a different argument.

Rebecca took a deep breath. Might as well get this over with. "Anyway, Adah wants me to come over to talk to her tomorrow, so Abner will pick me up at eleven."

Her brother's jaw clenched. "I can drive you over in the buggy."

"Abner thinks the car will be warmer." After spending time out there just now, Rebecca wasn't quite convinced. Being tucked under blankets with a hot water bottle when she rode in the buggy kept her body toasty warm even though her face froze.

"Riding with Abner is not necessarily safer." Jakob's tone was sharper than a knife edge. "I'm not sure I can trust Abner."

"He made one mistake, and all of you act as if he were a criminal," Rebecca burst out. "I thought you told him you forgave him."

Jakob stared down at his shoes. "I did. That doesn't mean I don't worry about you."

"Forgiveness means giving him another chance."

"I'm not so sure—" Jakob rubbed his chin and looked as if he planned to say more, but he glanced at the clock. "This will have to wait until another time." As he exited the kitchen bearing the two plates, he said over his shoulder, "I only want you to be safe. Please think about what I said."

Rebecca longed to retort she already had. At least as far as her safety, but as for her heart… That was a different matter.

After Rebecca went into the house, Abner sat in the driveway, staring at the closed front door. The door he'd dashed in and out of as a *youngie*, with Jakob on his heels. Even back then, he'd been enamored of Jakob's pretty younger sister. His interest had grown over the years as she'd been willing to accompany him on the escapades Jakob frowned at.

The two rebels had enjoyed each other's company until one day he'd fallen out of a tree and lay stunned on the ground. When he opened his eyes, Rebecca had knelt beside him, gazing anxiously down at him. After he assured her he was all right, only winded, she breathed a sigh of relief. And then her lips curved into that smile, the one that took his breath away, and he determined then and there that someday they'd marry.

Now that door had closed with a chilling finality. His foolish mistake had cost him the girl he loved. Now her parents didn't trust him, and neither did Rebecca. He'd do anything to undo the damage, but could he ever win back her heart?

At the moment, he didn't have time to try. Too many things demanded his attention. Maybe once he'd found a job and figured out his mother's treatment, he could convince Rebecca to court him again. Right now, he had to live with the hollow emptiness, the pain of losing her, while caring for his siblings and making sure *Mamm* received the best care possible.

Coming over here today had stirred memories best

buried. And that phone call? He fished his phone out of his pocket and mashed the On button. Why, after he'd put all that behind him, did they have to call him today? Rebecca would assume he'd been in contact with them and all his denial had been lies.

His finger hovered over the Delete button. It was rather odd that they'd called him. Maybe he should listen to the message to be sure they'd not run into any problems or hitches. If something bad had happened, he needed to know. He pressed the voicemail button instead.

Hey, Abner. Paul here. Look, we've been having some difficulties with authenticity while shooting the show. Would you be willing to come to New York for a few weeks to coach the actors? If they could hear your accent and all, it would help. I promise no in-front-of-camera work. Could you call back to let me know your decision? If you can't do it, I'll need to find someone else ASAP.

A long pause ensued, and Abner started to hit the Delete button when Paul continued, *Oh, forgot to tell you the pay.* He named a sum that took Abner's breath away.

Abner replayed the message twice to be sure he hadn't misheard. By helping out for a few weeks, he could earn more money than he could working here for a year. It seemed impossible.

He mulled it over as he backed out of Rebecca's driveway. *Mamm* wasn't well enough to cook or watch his younger brothers for extended periods of time, but if he could get someone to care for them…

Abner shook his head. He'd managed to disentangle himself from that sticky web of a TV-show contract.

No matter how much money they were offering, he'd be foolish to accept. And if he wanted Rebecca to ever consider dating him again, the less he had to do with that crew, the better off he'd be.

By the time he reached home, Abner had resolved to say *no* to the offer. Paul could be quite persuasive, so Abner prepared his speech ahead of time. Then he'd just decline any other offers Paul tendered.

Gathering his courage, Abner pushed redial. Paul answered on the first ring, almost as if he'd been sitting around waiting for this call. Abner's mouth had gone so dry, he could barely croak out a *hello* in response to Paul's cheery greeting.

"So glad you called, man," Paul said. "Herman's been going crazy here waiting for an answer. You know how antsy he gets."

"Yes, well, the thing is…" Abner's prepared speech slipped away. "Umm, well, my *mamm* has just been diagnosed with cancer, so I need to stay here to take care of her and watch my four younger brothers."

"Sorry to hear that." Paul's sympathy sounded genuine. "Would it help if we paid more money? Maybe you could afford to hire someone to take care of things for a short while?"

For a fleeting moment, the money danced before Abner's eyes. It would only be for a few weeks. Rebecca's face blotted out that picture. "I'm sorry. Wish I could help you, but I can't do it."

"More money?" Paul asked. "You drive a hard bargain."

"It's not the money. I need to be here for my family."

"I admire that," Paul said. "Has your mother started her treatments?"

"No, we just got the news." They hadn't even talked about that yet or about how they'd pay for them. Abner was dreading that conversation.

"Hope it goes well for her. Listen, I'd better get going to find somebody else. Herman was really counting on you." After a brief pause, Paul said, "You know anyone who'd be willing to do it?"

Abner could think of one or two guys his age that might agree, but he wouldn't feel right tempting them. They could easily end up in the same mess he had. "No, I don't think so. Sorry."

"Me too." Paul cleared his throat. "Tell your mom I'll be praying." He hung up before Abner could respond.

Abner forgot to turn off his phone. Instead, he sat there staring off into space. Surely he'd misheard that last sentence. Paul was less cynical than Herman, but they both were hard-edged New Yorkers, with no interest in God or religion. Had working on an Amish show changed them that much?

What would Paul think if he knew Abner wondered if he could trust the power of prayer?

Chapter Three

A little before eleven on Sunday, Rebecca and *Mamm* finished packing three wicker baskets with casseroles, loaves of homemade bread, desserts, and sandwiches.

"I hope this will help a little," *Mamm* said as she tucked a clean tea towel over one full basket. "Growing boys eat a lot."

"I know." As a teacher, Rebecca had seen her older scholars' voracious appetites. "It will be a start, at least. We can send over more later." She picked up two of the baskets and carried them to the front door.

Her mother followed with the other one. "I'm sure many women in the community will offer as well. I'll see about organizing meal drop-offs, as long as Betty doesn't mind."

Transitioning from bishop's wife after *Dat*'s stroke had been hard for *Mamm*. She'd gotten used to organizing events, but now all that seemed to be Betty Troyer's responsibility. And as the new bishop's wife, Betty preferred to be in charge.

"Maybe Betty would be grateful for some help overseeing the meal deliveries." Rebecca set her baskets beside the front door and couldn't resist peeking out to see if Abner had arrived.

"Perhaps." *Mamm* sounded doubtful as she thumped her basket down next to Rebecca's. One hand pressed to her back, *Mamm* straightened. "It doesn't matter who's in charge as long as the Lord's work gets done."

"True," Rebecca agreed, but she hid her smile.

Mamm laid a hand on Rebecca's shoulder. "Be sure to tell Adah we're praying for her."

"I certainly will," Rebecca assured her.

A car roared and rattled into the driveway. There was no mistaking Abner's junk heap, as he sometimes called it. Rebecca opened the door and waved.

Abner beamed at her as he pulled the car to a halt. He hopped out and hurried down the walkway toward her. Rebecca longed to keep staring at him, but she forced herself to bend and pick up two baskets.

When she stood, *Mamm* frowned and said in a low voice, "I hope this situation won't mean you'll be spending a lot of time together. Your *dat* and I would rather you two—" She stopped abruptly as Abner reached the front porch. "*Gude mariye*, Abner."

Abner greeted her *mamm* with a good morning too, before turning his attention to Rebecca. Sparks flew when their eyes met, and only *Mamm*'s throat clearing behind Rebecca broke the spell. She blinked and concentrated on the heavy wicker baskets in her hands. No need to get *Mamm* any more concerned than she already was.

"Let me take those from you." Abner reached for the baskets.

His hands brushed hers when he grasped the handles, and Rebecca sucked in a breath. Her pulse pattered so rapidly, she worried *Mamm* could tell.

"What is all this?" Abner asked, his voice not quite steady. Had he been as affected by that touch too?

"It's, umm…" Rebecca struggled to remember the contents of the baskets, but his biceps flexing under his shirt as he hefted the baskets arrested her attention.

"Food for your family." *Mamm*'s sharp tone rebuked Rebecca and snapped her out of her trance.

So did Abner's frown. Rebecca should have planned an explanation so Abner didn't view this as charity. She was grateful when *Mamm* intervened.

"Rebecca and I are worried about your *mamm*. If she's feeling poorly, surely she isn't well enough to cook meals. We're sending a little food to help her."

Abner's forehead stayed furrowed. "That's true, but—"

Mamm interrupted him. "The ladies of the church do this for anyone who's ill or had a new baby. Your *mamm* has done it many times for others. Now it's our turn to repay her."

Although he still didn't look mollified, Abner said, "*Danke* for your kindness." When Rebecca reached behind the door and lifted the third basket, his lips thinned, but he didn't protest. He tilted his head to indicate Rebecca should precede him down the walk.

Before she shut the door, *Mamm* called, "Please have Rebecca home before one. Her *aenti* and *onkel* will be visiting us this afternoon."

That was the first Rebecca had heard of any relatives visiting today. Had her parents—or Jakob—made those plans to prevent her from spending too much time with Abner?

Abner managed to hold his tongue until they reached the car, but as they stowed the three large baskets in the trunk, he said, "I don't want people feeling sorry for my family or me."

"I understand." Rebecca's gentle answer defused much of his irritation. "Like *Mamm* said, everyone in the community helps each other. It's your *mamm*'s turn now."

When she put it that way, it took some of the sting out of accepting charity. But the embarrassment of being jobless made it difficult to accept help graciously. The truth was, though, *Mamm* could barely struggle through the day. She would appreciate the meals.

As he started the engine, he couldn't help wondering if he should have given more thought to Paul's offer. He could have hired someone to come in to cook for them. Right now, he couldn't afford to turn down any help.

One glance at Rebecca's sweet face convinced him he'd made the right decision. He never wanted to hurt her again. And if he took the job with Paul and Herman, he couldn't look her in the eyes with a clear conscience.

"So how is your *mamm* doing?" Rebecca's question startled him from his thoughts.

"She's weak and spending more time in bed." He should at least thank Rebecca for her thoughtfulness. "I'm sure she'll appreciate you sending meals. It hasn't been easy for her to cook."

"I could come over some days after school to do a little cooking," she offered.

Picturing her in their kitchen making meals like a wife caused his stomach to do strange flips. He swallowed hard before answering. "*Danke*, but maybe we'd better not, um—" How did he phrase this?

Rebecca's cheeks flushed a becoming shade of pink. "I didn't mean…"

"I know you didn't. I just think it's better not to go there."

"I agree."

She hadn't been thinking along the same lines as he'd been, and now she'd agreed so quickly, it hurt. He kept hoping the breakup had been prompted by her parents, and she'd soon change her mind. Now he wasn't so sure.

After they arrived at the house and unloaded the baskets, Abner turned to Rebecca. "Would it be all right if I call my brothers for an early dinner?"

Mamm hadn't been feeling well this morning so they'd done the best they could foraging for breakfast. A task made more difficult because neither he nor *Mamm* had time to go grocery shopping this week.

"Of course. I'll put these things away in the refrigerator."

Abner jumped in front of her. "No, that's all right. I can do it." Once she saw their propane-powered refrigerator was practically empty, she'd be certain they were a charity case.

"Don't be silly." Rebecca sidestepped him and pulled open the door.

He expected her to turn pity-filled eyes in his direction, but she only slid the casserole dishes onto the shelves. "We couldn't go shopping this week because of all *Mamm*'s appointments."

"I see." Rebecca shut the door and returned to the table for more items. "I'm glad we brought a few things to last until you can get to the store."

Her matter-of-fact attitude helped ease some of his embarrassment. She also didn't point out that if he lost his job, next week might be the last time he could afford to grocery shop.

Abner went to the foot of the stairs and called to his brothers, who came thundering downstairs and into the kitchen. Rebecca had set a platter of ham-and-cheese sandwiches in the center of the table, and all four boys gazed at them hungrily.

"Help yourselves," Rebecca said, handing out plates from the cupboard.

Seeing her making herself at home in the kitchen again brought a lump to his throat. A few weeks ago, she'd been helping his *mamm* wash dishes, and some nights when she'd sneak out to meet him, they'd come here after everyone was in bed, and they'd sit at the table sharing a snack.

His brothers dove into the pile of sandwiches and grabbed large handfuls of chips from the bag she'd opened. Then they plopped down at the table, bowed their heads for prayer, and tore into the food while Rebecca circulated, handing out glasses of milk.

"Thanks, Reb," his youngest brother, Philip, said around a mouthful of food.

Abner winced, not only at his brother's talking with his mouth full but also at his use of the nickname Abner had given Rebecca. He'd teased her that "Reb" was short for "Rebel," not just "Rebecca." At the time, she'd laughed and told him she liked it. How did she feel about it now that she no longer planned to rebel?

Her face gave away nothing as she smiled at each of his brothers in turn. They all grinned back.

"We missed you," Philip mumbled around a mouthful of food. "Where have you been?"

"I, um…" Rebecca shot him a questioning glance as if unsure how to answer.

He hadn't told his brothers about their breakup, hoping not speaking about it would make it less painful. Now he regretted not being honest with them. He'd have to discuss this with them later. Right now he needed to rescue her.

"Rebecca's here to see *Mamm*, so why don't you finish your dinner while we take a plate in to her?"

Full mouths meant no answers, only nods from everyone around the table. Their eyes lit up, though, when Rebecca pulled out a pan of honey bars. She sliced them into generous squares and served one to each boy amid mumbled *danke*s and grateful glances.

When she raised her head, he added his own choked *danke* as a sharp pain knifed through his heart. He'd often envisioned their children crowded around a table like this, with her at his left side. A dream that might never come true.

"I'm ready," she said with a dazzling smile.

And for a second, he had no idea what she meant. Had she read his mind and was agreeing she was ready to be his wife? Then his spirits plummeted. Of course. She meant she was ready to see *Mamm*. He'd gotten carried away with his fanciful imaginings, something the bishop often warned against.

"*Mamm* will be glad to see you." He tried to keep his voice neutral and not betray the feelings welling up inside at the thought of a future together. "Should we take her a plate?"

Rebecca reached for another plate and placed a sandwich on it. When she picked up the knife to cut another honey bar, he stopped her. Ordinarily, his *mamm* loved sweets, but she hadn't had much of an appetite over the past few weeks.

"*Mamm* hasn't been eating much lately. Why don't we see how she does with the sandwich first?"

Rebecca nodded, poured a glass of milk, and followed him to the bedroom. He knocked on the door and, at *Mamm*'s weak *Come in*, pushed open the door.

"*Ach*, you've brought Rebecca with me here in bed?" She struggled to a sitting position, tugged at her work apron to straighten it, and ran a hand over her head as if to ensure her *kapp* was on straight. "Let me get to a chair."

Abner rushed around her side of the bed to assist her. She batted his hands away, but he ignored her futile efforts. He'd seen her struggle to get to her feet earlier that morning. She needed assistance whether she'd admit it or not.

A small voice in his head whispered, *Refusing to accept help when it's needed seems to be a family trait.*

The voice was right. He and his *mamm* disliked accepting assistance, but in this challenging situation, they might both be forced to give in.

* * *

Rebecca's eyes grew misty as Abner gently helped his *mamm* to a chair and supported her until she was settled. He had such a good heart. So many people only saw his rebellion and wrote him off as a troublemaker, but she'd seen the many sacrifices he'd made for his *mamm* and his siblings. That was only one of the many things she loved about him, but until he made the commitment to join the church, she couldn't even consider courting him.

When Adah had rearranged her skirt and apron, she made a shooing motion with her hand. "I'd like to be alone with Rebecca."

"Alone? But I thought—"

Adah pointed to the door. "Yes, alone," she said, her tone firm.

A look of hurt flashed in Abner's eyes before he turned and exited.

"Do me a favor, dear," Adah said. "Would you check to be sure Abner's not listening at the door?"

Rebecca gasped. "He wouldn't do that."

Adah chuckled. "I'm pleased with that answer. No, he wouldn't do that, but not many people believe that about him."

"Well, I know he's not what most people think he is."

"Even after he betrayed you with that TV audition?"

Abner had told his *mamm* about that?

"You seem surprised, Rebecca. Sons do need to explain to their *mamms* why they're no longer spending time with the girl they love." Adah peered at her closely. "But you haven't answered my question."

How did you tell your ex-boyfriend's *mamm* about

the depth of hurt that situation had left behind? But this was Adah, who'd been like a second mother to her. Rebecca struggled to put those feelings into words.

"Abner was acting strangely that night. He—we did things we'd never done before." Rebecca, her cheeks burning, bumbled through an explanation of dancing with him. Neither of them had ever danced. Nor had they ever been that close. She'd just stumbled along awkwardly in Abner's arms and been relieved when he suggested leaving.

Adah nodded. "Abner said the same thing. He feels guilty for that and for what happened next."

"I do too." Rebecca lowered her gaze to study the variegated patterns in the rag rug on the polished wooden floor. Would Abner's *mamm* make her recount the kissing too?

"You didn't suspect both of those were being filmed, did you?" Adah's voice was gentle, accepting.

"Of course not. I would never have agreed." Rebecca regretted her tone. "I'm sorry, I didn't mean to snap like that. It's only that I'm ashamed of what I did. Knowing someone was filming us made it even worse."

"I know. Abner's said many times he wishes he'd told you. If you'd reacted the way you just did now, he never would have done it."

Was Adah blaming her for not stopping Abner? That wasn't fair. She had no idea about the taping. But the truth of the matter was, if she'd been as adamant about not dancing or kissing as she'd just been about the filming, none of this would have happened. The production company would have had nothing to tape.

Rebecca pressed her hands to her hot cheeks and

hung her head. "I can see how my going along with everything made it worse. I should have said *no*."

Adah leaned forward. "I didn't say that to make you feel guilty or blame yourself. Abner takes full responsibility for pressuring you into doing it and for not telling you he was auditioning." She closed her eyes and winced.

"Are you all right?" Rebecca started to get out of her chair, but Adah waved her back to her seat.

"I'll be fine. Sometimes I get these pains. Not sure if it's the cancer or something else. I'm getting old, so it's to be expected."

"You're not old," Rebecca protested. Adah was only in her mid- to late-forties, and until recently, she'd been lively and active. Seeing her like this was hard. "How have you been feeling?"

"Not so good, but I'm grateful that God has seen fit to give me another day. I don't know how many more I have, though, so that's why I wanted to talk to you." She slumped back in the chair, alarming Rebecca.

Before Rebecca could get out of her seat, Adah opened her eyes. "I'm feeling very weak. Would you be able to help me back to bed?"

"Of course." Hurrying over, Rebecca helped her stand, but when they reached the bed, Adah couldn't get in. Rebecca wasn't sure she could lift her alone. "Should I call Abner?"

"No, no." Adah waved a hand weakly. "Just give me a minute."

Rebecca supported her until she was able to climb onto the bed. Once again, she straightened her clothing and checked her *kapp*. Adah should probably change into a nightgown, but if Rebecca suggested it, Adah would no doubt refuse. She'd follow the rule of not getting ready for bed until nightfall.

Adah motioned to the chair nearest the bed. "Could you drag that over here? I don't want anyone to hear what I have to say."

After Rebecca obliged and settled onto the chair, Adah reached out and grasped her arm. "I'm concerned about my family and what will happen when I'm gone."

"But you don't know that. They have treatments. People recover from cancer all the time."

"I don't intend to seek treatment."

"But—"

Adah held up a hand. "My mind is made up. If this is God's will, then I plan to accept it."

"You don't think God would approve of getting treatments?"

Adah closed her eyes. "I'm not willing to put that burden on my family." Her eyes popped open. "Please don't tell Abner I said that, or he'll try to insist. I don't want his last memories of me to be of us arguing."

"Jakob is already planning a fundraiser, and the church will help." Because they didn't believe in insurance, the church had a fund to help cover medical expenses. Everyone contributed what they could.

"A fundraiser can pay only a small fraction of the cost, and I won't drain church funds for expensive treatments that may not even work."

"What about Mexico? Everyone says it's cheaper there."

"I'm feeling too weak to make a thirty-five-hour trip."

"You wouldn't have to do it all at once. They'd stop along the way, and you could stay with relatives or other Amish families."

Adah shook her head. "I'm leaving it up to God whether or not He chooses to heal me."

Rebecca couldn't argue with that, but would God want her to accept help?

Adah slumped against the backboard of the bed, looking weak and drained.

Rebecca reached for the food she'd brought in earlier. "Would you like to eat a little or have a sip of milk?"

"A little milk please." After she'd taken a few sips, she motioned for Rebecca to set the glass back on the nightstand. "While I still have the strength to do this, I want to get some things settled for the future. That's why I asked Abner to get you."

Her words confused Rebecca. What did she have to do with Adah's planning for the future?

"We didn't finish our conversation about the filming. Have you forgiven Abner?"

"Of course. I told him that the night we, um, I—"

"Broke up with him?" Adah suggested.

Rebecca nodded. "Yes, I told him that then."

"Do you still love him?" Adah leaned closer and studied Rebecca.

With all my heart. But she couldn't say that to his *mamm.*

"Never mind. You don't need to answer that. I can tell from your expression the answer is *yes,* and that's good."

Rebecca was growing more confused by the minute.

What difference did it make whether or not she loved Abner? Before she could ask, Adah nodded.

"I have a favor to ask. I may not be here much longer, but I'd like to have one thing settled before I go. You love Abner, and he loves you. I've always believed you're the one for him, and now that Abner says you've gotten right with God and plan to join the church, I hope you'll stay together."

Unlike Rebecca's parents, Adah had always encouraged Rebecca and Abner to spend time with each other. She'd raised no opposition to them being together, even though they shouldn't have been dating until they were with the church.

As much as she'd like to agree with Adah's request, Rebecca had to decline, unless Abner made a decision to turn his life over to God. "Abner says he'll take baptismal classes in the spring with me. If he does and we both join the church, then I can date him. But not until then."

Adah sighed. "I was afraid of that, but you're right. You should abide by the rules. Could you at least promise me you'll stay close to him, nudge him in the right direction so he doesn't stray too far?"

Rebecca stared at her, unsure how to answer. She'd promised her parents not to spend time with Abner. Now that she'd confessed to her family and gotten right with the Lord, she intended to honor her parents.

"Right now, he's uncertain about his faith, but I know he'll come around. You, of everyone, have the biggest influence on him. Will you use that influence to help him stay on the right path?"

She had no idea how she'd reconcile this with what

her parents expected. But how could she deny what might be Adah's dying request? "I'll do my best."

"Danke." Adah squeezed Rebecca's hand. "You've eased my mind considerably. With a few nudges from you, I know he'll take baptism classes and join the church. Then he can officially court you. No more of this sneaking around."

Suddenly, Adah wilted back against the pillows. She closed her eyes, and her skin paled.

Alarmed, Rebecca leaned over her. "Are you all right?"

"I'm only tired." It seemed to be a great effort for her to open her eyes, but when she did, she pinned Rebecca with a blazing look. "Will you also…promise me"—her breath came in gasps—"that the two of you will take good care of the boys?"

Rebecca gulped. First of all, she had no guarantee Abner would ever join the church or that they'd marry. And next, it had never occurred to her she'd have an instant family of four boys if they did marry. Three of his younger brothers were all her students in school, and she got along well with them, but she'd never thought about herself being a mother to them.

But with Adah's eyes boring into hers, she gave the only answer she could. "I promise."

Chapter Four

Abner paced outside *Mamm*'s room. What could they be talking about all this time? He had to get Rebecca back by one o'clock, and he'd hoped to spend some time with her first. He doubted her parents would let her come back again.

He wanted to lean close to the door to hear what they were discussing, but he refused to give in to temptation. Instead, he strode back and forth, just out of hearing range.

One thing Abner hoped was that Rebecca could talk *Mamm* into accepting treatment. *Mamm* insisted she didn't want to waste the money. Abner didn't care how much it cost, or even if it took the rest of his life to pay off. He wanted her to have the best care possible.

He'd been pacing for about half an hour when his cell phone buzzed. Not Paul again. Wasn't his refusal yesterday enough? Paul had said he'd give him time to think it over, but Abner needed none. He'd given his final answer yesterday.

He hurried into the kitchen so his conversation

couldn't be overheard by *Mamm*, and especially by Rebecca. She'd be upset if she knew he was speaking to Paul. At least it wasn't Paul's boss, Herman, who had a reputation for being volatile and unpredictable. Not that it mattered. Neither of them could convince him to come to New York. Abner had had a brief taste of stardom. That had taught him a hard lesson. A lesson he never wanted to repeat.

He caught the phone on the fifth ring. "Hello?"

"Thought you were never going to answer." Paul's cheerful, upbeat voice came over the line, suave and self-assured. "Hey, after we talked yesterday, I did some checking, and I've found a few ways to sweeten the pot."

"Huh?" He doubted that Paul had taken up cooking, but the only sweeteners he could think of were sugar and honey. And honey reminded him of Rebecca. He jerked his mind back to the conversation.

"Sweeten the pot means make a better deal. You get it now?"

Sometimes it seemed the movie people spoke a different language. "I guess so, but I don't think the pot needs sweetening. I already gave you my answer yesterday. I can't do it."

"But you haven't heard my news. Get this. There's a hospital nearby doing clinical trials on cancer. The techniques they're using are experimental, but they're already showing promising results."

"Sounds great, but it's probably very expensive."

"No, it's free," Paul said.

"Free?" There had to be some catch.

"It's a clinical trial," Paul repeated. "They need people willing to try it. I asked them about your mother.

They'd need to see her medical records and do an exam, but if she fits the profile they need to match, she's in. You can do most of the initial intake stuff online. You got access to a computer?"

"*Jah.* I mean yes." One of his former drag racing friends had one. The local library also had computers, but he'd prefer to have John's oversight and explanations.

"Awesome! Here's the site address." Paul rattled off names and dot com.

"Can you repeat that?" Abner grabbed a notebook and pencil from his brother's backpack to jot down the letters Paul recited. Then he read it back.

"Here's the plan. Your mom needs to be there on Tuesdays and Thursdays."

"Wait a minute," Abner objected. "She hasn't even agreed to it, and neither have I. Even if we both agreed, we have no idea if she'd be accepted."

"Fair enough. Let's go hypothetical here. Suppose she is accepted. She needs to be checked by those two days. We'll take care of transportation and housing from Monday night through Friday morning. You can go home for long weekends."

"I assume you're not doing this out of the goodness of your heart?"

"Well, there is one tiny catch. You'd have to work for us from Tuesday to Thursday."

"I see." But his feelings on that hadn't changed. Would *Mamm* still be able to do the clinical trial if he turned this down? He'd have John check that out. New York was a three-hour train ride, so hopefully the trip wouldn't be too taxing for her.

"Good. So it's a deal?" Paul sounded elated.

"I didn't agree to anything yet."

Paul's sigh shook the phone. "What else do you need? Herman's getting impatient."

In the background behind Paul, a loud voice shouted, "You get this thing nailed down yet?"

"Not quite," Paul said. "Give me a few more minutes."

"I have two objections. One, I have four younger brothers, and—"

"That figures." Paul blew out an exasperated breath. "We'll pay for a nanny or a babysitter, whatever that costs."

"But the main reason," Abner continued, "is that I don't want to do it. I don't want to be involved with the TV show."

"What'd he say?" Herman yelled in the background.

"He said he's not going to do it."

"What!" Herman's screech was so loud, Abner moved the phone away from his ear. Even so, Herman's babbled threats came through loud and clear. Paul tried to calm him, but finally Herman snatched the phone away.

"You'll come to New York immediately," Herman barked. "I'm done with this namby-pamby stuff Paul's trying to pull."

Abner winced and held the phone an arm's length away from his ear. Herman's screaming still carried.

"You can have whatever Paul offered, but not a penny more." Herman cleared his throat with a loud hocking noise. "But here's the rest of the deal. *My* deal. If you don't come to New York like Paul asked starting next week, I'm going to include the video of you and Rebecca in my first TV show."

Abner grabbed the nearest chairback to hold himself up while the room whirled around him. They'd promised to destroy that audition. "You broke your agreement?" he asked, his voice flat.

"Look, kid, this is show biz. Never trust anything that's not in writing. And even then, be suspicious. People are always out to knife you in the back."

"But—but—"

"Paul will be in touch tomorrow with the rest of the details, but I expect you here on Tuesday."

"I have to work on Tuesday." It was his last week. He owed Myron at least that much.

"See ya Tuesday, or else." The phone clicked off.

Sinking onto the chair, Abner let his phone fall onto the tabletop. Then he lowered his head into his hands. What was he going to do? If he didn't go, he'd ruin Rebecca's reputation. He cared little about his own; that was already in tatters. And how could he possibly let her know the film hadn't been destroyed?

"Abner?" Rebecca entered the kitchen to find him with his head down. "Are you all right?" First his *mamm*, and now him. The news seemed to be weighing them both down.

Slowly, he lifted his head and met her gaze with haunted eyes.

"What's wrong?"

He stared off into the distance. "I can't talk about it yet. I need some time to figure out what I'm going to do."

"I see." He looked so distressed, she wanted to reach out and touch him, reassure him everything would be all right. But she had no way of knowing whether or not it would be. "I need to go, so I can get home on time."

He pushed himself to his feet. "I'm sorry. I should have been watching the clock."

"It's not your fault. I stayed in there with your *mamm* for so long."

He seemed to jolt back to the room with a start. "What did you talk about?"

"Lots of things." Rebecca wasn't about to tell him his mother wanted her to keep an eye on him, convince him to join the church, marry her, and share the parenting of his siblings.

"Did she discuss any treatment options with you?" he asked as they headed down the hall to the front door. He took her coat from a wall peg and handed it to her. If things had been different, he'd have helped her put it on, but he couldn't take a chance of touching her. Then he donned his own coat.

Rebecca hesitated to tell him his *mamm*'s plan, but perhaps he already knew. "She intends to refuse treatment."

"That's what she told me, but why?"

With his eyes lasering into hers, demanding an answer, Rebecca fumbled for words. "She said she's trusting God."

"A lot of good that'll do her."

Rebecca was so shocked, her mouth flew open, and she struggled to close it. He couldn't mean that, could he? From time to time, he'd expressed doubts about

God, but to say something like this, his disbelief must run deep.

"I'm sorry, Rebecca." Abner's tone was conciliatory.

"You don't need to apologize to me," she said. Although she tried to keep the censure from her tone, she wasn't successful. "You need to ask God's forgiveness."

"I'm not sure." He looked away, then dropped his gaze to the floor. "After what happened to *Dat*, my job, and *Mamm*, I find it hard to believe God hears us."

"Of course he does."

"He didn't listen when I begged him to save *Dat*."

"Oh, Abner, I know how hard that was, but God's divine will is working even there. We can't always see the purpose at the time, but we still need to trust Him."

Abner muttered something under his breath that she didn't catch. She was pretty sure it wasn't words of agreement.

Adah was right, he did need someone to nudge him toward God. She'd promised to be that person, but for now, she'd pour out her concerns in prayer.

"*Mamm* definitely said she wouldn't allow any treatments?" Abner opened the front door, and the wind roared in. "Why don't you stay behind me, and I'll try to block the wind?"

"*Danke.* I think she's worried about the cost." Rebecca clapped a hand over her mouth. Had Adah said not to tell Abner? Rebecca couldn't remember for sure. That part of the conversation was hazy.

Abner stopped so abruptly, she almost plowed into him. He whirled around to face her. "Did she say that, or are you only guessing?"

If she should have been keeping that info to herself,

it was too late now to repair the damage. "I don't think your *mamm* wanted you to know that. She doesn't want to burden you."

"She'd never be a burden, but if that's her only objection, I might have a solution." He turned and headed toward the car. His trudging of a few moments ago had transformed into bouncing, joyful steps. "I just heard of a free treatment."

"Free?" Rebecca tried to keep disbelief from seeping into her voice, but she didn't quite succeed.

"I don't blame you for being skeptical," Abner said as he held open the car door for her. "I didn't believe it at first, but I plan to check it out."

"That would be *wunderbar*, if it's true." She was pretty sure Adah would agree to a free treatment program. Would she consider it a sign from God? Rebecca slid into the car seat and bit back a yelp. The fake leather seats were icier than the air outside.

"I'll warm it up," Abner promised as he shut her door. He hurried around the car and turned on the engine. Chilly air blasted from the dashboard. "Let me turn that off until the engine heats up."

They shivered their way through several blocks before he turned on the heat. Only a trickle of air came out, but not enough to warm them. Abner banged on the dashboard, then fiddled with buttons and dials trying to get more heat.

Her teeth chattering, Rebecca asked, "Where is the free treatment program? Somewhere local?"

"Um, no. It's out of state." After she shot him a questioning glance, he added, "New York," in a defensive tone.

"How in the world did you find out about it?"

A sickish look passed over Abner's face. "I heard about it from someone." His eyes begged her not to ask more questions.

But Abner's hesitation raised a burning question, one Rebecca had to know the answer to. "Who is this *someone*?"

Abner remained silent until they stopped at a red light. Then he squeezed his eyes shut for a moment. "I'd really rather not get into it." He didn't want her to know he'd reconnected with the producer and his assistant. Even worse, he never wanted her to know about the film. They'd both assumed it had been destroyed, and he planned to see it happened this time. Whatever it took.

But she appeared determined to find out the truth. "An acquaintance from New York, by any chance?"

Abner took his foot off the brake and coasted through the green light. "Please, Rebecca, can we just let this drop?"

"If you won't tell me, then I'll make a guess. Did either of them happen to be named Herman or Paul?"

He'd promised himself he wouldn't lie to her. Reluctantly, he nodded.

"Which one?" Her *hands-on-her-hips* tone made it clear she'd keep digging until she discovered the answers.

"Paul."

"He called you yesterday, didn't he?" At Abner's nod, she fired off more questions. "Why would Paul suggest a cancer program? How did he know about your *mamm*? Have the two of you been in touch since they left Lancaster?"

Abner held up a hand to stop the inquisition. "I can only answer one at a time. I haven't seen or talked to Paul since he was at Sarah's house last month. That is, until yesterday. He called me for the first time when we were together."

"You didn't answer the call because you didn't want to talk to him in front of me." She pinned him with the fury in her eyes.

"It wasn't like that. I turned off the phone, intending to delete his call." If only he had, he wouldn't be in this mess. If they hadn't reached him, they'd have found someone else. But now that they had, they'd managed to blackmail him.

"But you didn't delete it." The disappointment in her eyes slashed through him.

"I don't know why I listened to the message, but I did. They wanted me to come to New York to work for them." Rebecca sucked in a sharp breath, but Abner kept going. He wanted her to know this part of the story. "I called Paul back to tell him *no*. That's when I mentioned *Mamm*."

"I'm so glad you told him *no*." Rebecca accompanied that sentence with a brilliant smile. One that took his breath away. One that reminded him why he fell in love with her. One he didn't deserve.

Could he leave things like this? With Rebecca smiling? He'd told her the whole truth up until this point. Was it lying to withhold additional facts? Although his conscience answered *yes*, his ego begged him to remain silent.

Chapter Five

❧

Neither of them said a word as they drove the last few blocks to Rebecca's neighborhood. Abner wrestled with his conscience, but it refused to yield to temptation. As they turned onto her street, truth won the battle.

"Rebecca?" Gripping the steering wheel, he forced himself to say, "There's more to the story." Then he waited until he had her full attention before continuing.

"Paul called back this morning while you were talking to *Mamm*. That's when he told me about this experimental cancer program."

"How nice of him." Rebecca beamed. "Sarah said he took a Bible with him when he left her house, so they've been praying he'll find his way back to the Lord."

Abner ran one finger around his collar, which suddenly seemed to be choking him. "I don't know about any of that, but I was grateful to learn about the treatment program."

"So am I, and I hope your *mamm* will agree to go. I feel like this is a perfect opportunity sent from God."

Would she still feel that way if she knew the whole

story? Abner squirmed in his seat, wishing once again he could end the account at this point, but he plunged on. "Paul also begged me to come and work for them. He offered to pay transportation and housing expenses if I did."

"I hope you didn't agree." Rebecca studied his heated cheeks. "You did, didn't you?"

Abner pretended to be fascinated by the snow-covered corn stubble in her neighbor's field, while he tried to compose an answer, one that sounded both understandable and believable. In the end, he settled on the truth. "Yes, I did."

Rebecca stared at Abner, uncertain she'd heard him right. Had he just said he'd be working for the TV producers?

They'd pulled into her driveway, but Rebecca didn't get out. She intended to stay in this car until she had answers. Was this why Adah had asked to see her? Did she have a suspicion that Abner planned to get involved with the TV industry again? But Paul hadn't called until she was talking to Abner's *mamm*.

Her throat tight, she said, "I hope I misunderstood you. You couldn't possibly have said you were going to work for them."

"I did," he said miserably.

"How could you? Especially after what happened to us before. You'd sell your integrity for money?"

"It wasn't the money. I turned that down. But when he said he'd help with *Mamm*—"

"You don't need Paul to get into the treatment program, do you?"

Abner shook his head. "No, but—"

"Good, then once you see about getting her enrolled or whatever they call it, you can use the money from Jakob's fundraiser to pay for transportation and housing. If you need more funds, the church will cover it."

"I thought about doing that, but there's more."

She crossed her arms and trained an ice-cold stare in his direction. She couldn't believe he'd give in to those crooks. He'd said it wasn't about money, but what else could it be? He'd already admitted he didn't need Paul to get his mom into the treatment program.

Abner's eyes begged for understanding. "Herman got on the phone and pressured me into saying yes, because—"

Rebecca didn't want to hear any more excuses. She held up a hand. Adah had said Abner would listen to her if she stuck to her principles. Now was a good time to put that to the test. "I don't want you going to New York."

He groaned. "You don't understand. I have to."

"No, you don't. You can call them back and tell them you won't do it."

Abner shook his head. "I have no choice. Besides, I've already promised them I'd come. You know what the Bible says about giving your word."

Rebecca couldn't argue with that. Scripture did say you should not break your word, but he'd made an agreement he never should have made. Rebecca left the car and headed for the house, her spirit crushed.

His heart heavy, Abner waited until she'd made it safely into the house before pulling away. He wished he could have walked her to the door, but her stiff posture made it clear she wouldn't welcome his assistance. Something in the way she'd walked away told him he had no chance for the future, not even if he joined the church.

"I'm doing this for you," he whispered. He'd save her reputation, but she'd never know. And this time, he'd make sure he destroyed the film himself. Otherwise, how many more times would Herman use it to blackmail him?

He hadn't even had a chance to explain to Rebecca that he wouldn't be in front of the camera. Would that have made a difference? Softened her reaction a little? He doubted he'd have a chance to find out. Most likely she'd never speak to him again.

When he arrived home, *Mamm* had already fallen asleep. He'd have to wait until she woke to discuss the situation with her. He hoped she'd agree to go all the way to New York for treatments.

Abner sank onto a chair at the kitchen table. He reached for one of the sandwiches Rebecca had brought earlier. The tang of mustard on his tongue reminded him of one of their secret picnics. He'd brought root beer, and she'd brought ham sandwiches just like these. And they'd held hands and— He shook his head to clear the memories.

As suppertime approached, *Mamm* was still napping. Abner was grateful for the casseroles Rebecca had brought. He slid one into the oven before he joined his brothers in the barn to milk the cows and feed the animals.

The warm, steamy room scented with the aroma of bubbling Yumasetti casserole welcomed them back to the house. They washed up and enjoyed the hearty hamburger-and-noodle dish. By the time they were done and his two younger brothers were washing the dishes, *Mamm* had awoken. He carried a small plate into her room.

She struggled to sit up in bed. Abner rushed over to help, but she waved him away. Once she was upright, he tucked extra pillows behind her, then handed her the plate.

The half-finished sandwich and partially full milk glass made him sad. Like most Amish families, *Mamm* had always insisted they clean their plates. No one ever left even a tiny scrap on the plate. The fact that *Mamm* had not eaten every bite revealed how ill she was despite all her efforts to downplay it.

She picked up the fork he handed her and lifted a small tidbit to her mouth. He wished he could offer to feed her, but she'd never allow it.

Abner took a deep breath. "*Mamm*, I heard about a cancer treatment program today that's—"

Mamm shook her head. "As I told Rebecca today, I'm leaving it up to God. If he chooses to heal me, that's His will."

"Rebecca believes this opportunity is from God. Will you at least let me tell you about it?"

His *mamm*'s lips pressed into a thin line. "I don't see any point when I won't be considering it."

Ignoring her frown, Abner continued, "This program is experimental, so it's free." Was that a flicker of interest in *Mamm*'s eyes? "The only problem is it's in New York, but I've been offered a job that includes free transportation and housing for the three days a week we'd need to go."

She looked at him suspiciously but chewed thoughtfully as he described the arrangements. Yet, when he finished, she shook her head.

"That's a generous offer from your company, but I can't accept."

"If you won't do it for yourself, do it for others."

Mamm frowned. "What do you mean?"

"Being part of the experiment would help researchers find cures for cancer. Who knows how many people's lives you could save? Would you let others die?"

Her lips trembled. "*Neh*, I could never do that."

"Your own children need you too. You still have four young boys to raise." He needed her too, but the little ones needed her more.

She set down her fork and squeezed her eyes shut. Several teardrops sparkled on her eyelashes. "I'm not sure I have the strength to travel that far."

"I'll be with you to help you."

"And what about the boys? I can't leave them alone here."

"They offered to pay for a nanny, if we needed one."

"They? Who's this *they*? You haven't told me anything about this job of yours that's willing to take care of me too. And how did you get a job in New York? Will you need to move there?"

Abner gulped. He'd been hoping to avoid this part of the discussion. *Mamm* would most likely react the same way Rebecca had. "Well, first of all, I won't need to move to New York. I'll be there the same days you are.

We can ride on the train together and both stay in the apartment. The job is only temporary, but it pays well."

"And you'll be doing what for this job?"

"Sort of consulting work," he mumbled, waving a hand vaguely in the air.

"What kind of consulting? And for who?"

"Well, maybe, more like teaching. For people who want to know more about the Amish." He hoped that would satisfy her, but he worried it might not.

"Abner!" The sharp edge in his *mamm*'s voice reflected her annoyance at his evading her questions. "Who are you working for?"

He couldn't look her in the eye, so he concentrated on his hands, which he'd clenched in his lap. "The TV producer."

Mamm closed her eyes, and her head sank back on the pillow. "Oh, Abner."

"I'm not going to be filmed. I'm only going to teach the actors how to speak with an accent."

Her lips moved soundlessly, as if she were praying. Then she opened her eyes, and her sorrowful expression piled more guilt onto the heap he already carried.

"I had to do it," Abner explained. He filled her in on Herman's threat and the undestroyed film. "I can't let anyone see that tape of Rebecca. It would destroy her reputation."

Her eyes filled with tears, *Mamm* nodded. "You made a foolish mistake, but it seems as if it may follow you the rest of your life. And Rebecca too." She tilted her head to look him straight in the eye. "Does Rebecca know?"

"About the job, *yes*. But not about the film." He hastened to add, "And I don't want her to know."

"How did she react?" *Mamm* studied his face.

"I don't think she'll ever speak to me again." Abner tried not to reveal the depth of his hurt as he spoke, but *Mamm*'s knowing look told him she'd read the pain under his words.

"I'd hoped the two of you would work things out, but this certainly makes it difficult, if not impossible, especially if you don't want to tell her the whole truth." *Mamm*'s sigh seemed to come from the depth of her being.

Abner had already reached that conclusion. Not telling Rebecca the truth had cost him their relationship. Now he'd compounded it by hiding something else from her, but he didn't want to upset her. And last time, he'd been so caught up in his own thoughts of stardom, he hadn't considered Rebecca's feelings. This time, he'd put her feelings first and thought only of protecting her, but he'd lost her anyway.

Mamm met Rebecca at the front door. "How is Adah?"

"Very weak and tired." Rebecca turned away from her *mamm*'s searching glance as she hung up her coat and bonnet. She tried to keep her hands steady so they wouldn't reveal her agitation. How could Abner have taken a job with Paul and Herman?

"Merv and Maria will be here shortly to have dinner with us," *Mamm* said behind her. "You didn't eat at the Lapps', did you?"

"No, I didn't have time. I spent the whole time with Adah."

"You didn't have any time with Abner?" *Mamm*'s question carried a touch of censure.

Rebecca's hand jerked, sending her bonnet tumbling to the floor. She bent and picked it up, wishing *Mamm* would retreat to the kitchen and allow her a little time to compose herself. But *Mamm* continued to hover, waiting for a response.

"No." Rebecca's denial came out too sharp and too terse, making it sound as if she were lying. "We only saw each other on the ride over and back." She pivoted and headed to the kitchen before *Mamm* could examine her face. "Look, I'm never going to date Abner, so you don't have anything to worry about."

"I see." *Mamm* sounded uncertain as she followed Rebecca down the hall.

Rebecca regretted speaking so harshly, but if she tried to apologize, she'd burst into tears. She couldn't believe Abner would go back to New York. He must really have been enamored of show business. And his mother had been wrong. Rebecca had no influence on Abner. He still intended to go to New York even after she raised her objections.

Despite the breakup, Rebecca had been harboring hopes that Abner would turn his life around, surrender his life to God, and join the church so they could be together. He'd dashed all her dreams. Once he got involved in big-city life, he'd never be content to come back to their quiet farmlands. And she feared living in New York would make him forget her—and God.

Chapter Six

When Rebecca got home the next day after school, several women were gathered in the living room. *Mamm* motioned for her to come join the group. Rebecca was tired after a sleepless night followed by a long day of teaching, but she had to be polite.

"We're planning how to help the Lapps. We'll take meals over, of course, but she'll need people to watch the boys when she's at her treatments." *Mamm* beamed at her. "You went to see Adah yesterday. Did she say when her treatments begin?"

Rebecca didn't feel right revealing Adah's decision to a roomful of women, and she had no idea if Abner had convinced her to go to New York. "I don't know her plans yet."

Rebecca could practically see the questions forming in *Mamm*'s mind. *If you spent all that time with Adah, surely you'd know her plans. Was yesterday a ruse to spend more time with Abner?*

Rebecca shook her head in response to *Mamm*'s un-answered questions. But the suspicion in *Mamm*'s eyes cut Rebecca to the core, although it was justified, because months ago she had sneaked out of the house to meet Abner. If only she could erase the past and restore *Mamm*'s trust in her, but that would take time.

Sarah's *mamm* spoke up. "I pass the Lapps' on the way home. I can stop in and find out Adah's plans. Perhaps we could meet tomorrow to decide on a schedule."

The other women rose and donned cloaks and bonnets. Amid a flurry of thanks, they exited. Then *Mamm* turned to her, and the questions Rebecca had imagined became a reality.

"Yesterday you claimed you spent all your time with Adah. I'm wondering what you talked about." *Mamm*'s casual tone did not match the intensity of her eyes.

"About the past, what happened between Abner and me, her concerns about the future." Rebecca shrugged. "Nothing special. I tried to get her to eat or drink something. That was about it."

"I'm sure you understand, *dochder*, why I'm asking this."

"Yes, I do, but don't worry. I won't have anything more to do with Abner."

"I pray that's true."

Rebecca did too. For her own well-being, she planned to stay as far away from him as she could. Which should be easy if he headed to New York. But part of her regretted letting Adah down. The dream they both had of Abner marrying Rebecca had crumbled.

Someone tapped on the back door, and Rebecca turned from the sink filled with dishwater to see Sarah silhouetted in the window. Surprised, she hurried to the door.

"Come in, come in," she said as wintery winds blasted through the door. "It's freezing out there."

"It definitely is." Sarah removed her ice-covered gloves and blew on her reddened fingers.

"I guess you're here to see Jakob?" Rebecca turned to go and get her brother, but Sarah caught her arm.

"Actually, I came to speak to you and your *mamm*." She blushed. "I wouldn't mind seeing Jakob afterward, of course."

"I'll get *Mamm*." Rebecca gestured toward the table. "Have a seat. Oh, and help yourself to shoofly pie."

"*Danke*, but we just finished supper."

Her parents and Jakob were sitting in the living room, lit only by the faint light streaming down the hallway from the propane lamp Rebecca had been using to wash dishes. As she scurried down the hall, their faint conversation died. They must have been talking about her.

"Sarah's here," she announced.

Jakob jumped to his feet and glanced toward the front door. "I didn't hear her knock."

"She came to the back door." She stopped her brother before he could race down the hall. "She's here to talk to *Mamm* and me." She couldn't resist teasing Jakob a bit by not giving him the whole message.

His face fell, and he sank back on the couch.

"Don't worry," Rebecca assured him, "she agreed to talk to you after we're done."

His face lit up. "If she came to the back door, it probably means she cut across the fields. She'll need a ride home."

Rebecca laughed. "I expect that was her plan." She

left her brother humming a hymn from the *Ausbund* and joined *Mamm* in the kitchen. "Sarah, I believe someone wants to drive you home."

Her best friend's radiant smile warmed the room. "I would appreciate that."

"I'll just finish the last few dishes while we talk." Rebecca returned to the sink.

"The reason I'm calling," Sarah began, "is because when my *mamm* stopped by, Adah had a special request."

"Of course," *Mamm* said. "Whatever she needs, we'd be happy to do."

"Well, this is a bit unusual. She's decided to do the experimental treatments in New York."

"New York?" *Mamm* sounded puzzled. "I've heard of people going to Mexico, but not New York."

"It is rather unusual," Sarah agreed. "But evidently Abner has a job in New York, and he's found a medical center nearby that is doing clinical trials of a new treatment. Adah has agreed to try it, which means it's free."

"The free part sounds *wunderbar*," *Mamm* said, "but isn't it risky?"

"According to Abner, the results have been exceptionally positive so far."

Each time Sarah mentioned Abner's name, a stab of pain went through Rebecca's heart. She was grateful to have her back to the others.

"What will she do with the children then? Do we need to organize—"

"No, that's all taken care of. My cousin Esther recently suffered a heartbreak and came to visit. She'll be happy to have a job so she won't have to return to upstate New York for a while. She can care for the boys and cook meals for the family."

"What does Adah need us to do then?" *Mamm* sounded a bit disappointed.

"Actually," Sarah said in her usual conciliatory tone, "Adah would like Rebecca to accompany her to New York and stay with her during the testing the next few days."

The dish Rebecca was washing slipped through her hands and splashed into the dishwater, sloshing suds up over the edge of the sink and onto her black work apron. *Adah wants me to come to New York? But that means riding on the train with Abner. Spending time with him in the evenings.* No, that was asking too much.

Behind her, *Mamm* sucked in a breath. "I don't think…"

"I couldn't." Rebecca spun around to face them. "They'll be going during the week. I have to teach." She was grateful for the excuse.

The worry wrinkles on *Mamm*'s face smoothed out. "Of course. I'm sure Adah will understand Rebecca isn't available during the work week."

"That's why I came," Sarah said, "to let you know that I'm happy to substitute for as long as you need me, and Faithe Beiler offered to take my place as assistant teacher. The school board met and approved it already."

Rebecca blinked. How could they have arranged all this without checking with her? "But I can't do this."

"I'm not sure I want Rebecca going to New York. It's not safe."

Did *Mamm* mean going to the city or traveling with Abner? Perhaps both. Rebecca was more concerned about spending extended time with Abner. It had been hard enough cutting off the relationship, but in New York her resolve would be tested every day, every hour, every minute they were together.

"I understand it might be a little awkward."

A little awkward? Try totally, completely awkward. Uncomfortable. Unnerving. And tempting.

Rebecca couldn't allow herself to get sucked into this situation. But she didn't see any graceful way to avoid it.

"Everything is settled. Abner purchased three train tickets for tomorrow. They'll pick you up at six a.m. Adah's scheduled for her first tests tomorrow afternoon."

Only one strangled word made it past Rebecca's lips. "Tomorrow?"

"Yes, tomorrow. You'll need to pack for the three days. Adah said she'd be coming back early Friday morning."

Three days?

Mamm's mouth opened and closed, but no words came out.

"If I can help in any way, please let me know." Sarah glanced from one to the other, seemingly unfazed by the shock on both faces. "I'll just run in and say a quick good night to Jakob, if that's all right."

When no one answered, she headed for the living room.

Coming out of her trance, Rebecca wiped up the spilled suds and followed her friend down the hall. "Please, Sarah, I can't possibly do this. You know how awful our breakup was. You were there."

Sarah patted her arm. "I remember, and I realize it

was excruciating for you. I wish we could work out another solution, but Adah was adamant that she wouldn't go unless you accompanied her."

"You don't understand. Yesterday—"

"Ask for God's help, dear friend, and He'll see you through."

"Sarah!" Jakob came rushing out of the living room. "I thought I heard your voice."

The two of them stood there besotted, gazing into each other's eyes as Jakob reached out and entwined his fingers with Sarah's. She stared up at him with adoration.

"Let me take you home," Jakob said. "I don't want you walking in the dark."

"You don't have to," Sarah answered in a breathy voice.

"I want to," he insisted.

Rebecca turned her back and headed for the kitchen. If she and Abner were still together, she probably would have smiled at the sweetness of the love-struck couple, but right now, it only made her heart ache with loneliness.

In the early morning grayness, Abner stowed two bags in the trunk and turned on the engine so the interior would warm up, while *Mamm* gave Esther last-minute instructions. Then he assisted her out to the car and settled her in the backseat so she could stretch out her legs. After he tucked several blankets around her, he got behind the wheel.

Rebecca's suitcase already sat on the front porch when they pulled into her driveway. Abner climbed out, tapped lightly at the front door, and took her bag to the trunk. When Rebecca emerged in her coat and bonnet, she took his breath away, or maybe it was only the cold air constricting his lungs.

Either way, he could barely speak when he slid into the driver's seat with her beside him. He wished he'd put *Mamm* up front instead. The ride to the station would be uncomfortable.

"*Danke* for coming," he said.

She nodded and replied, "You're welcome," without once glancing in his direction.

"I appreciate you coming with me, Rebecca," his *mamm* said from the backseat. "Abner can't stay with me during the testing, so it will be nice to have company, and I always enjoy talking to you."

Though her lips pinched together at the mention of his name, Rebecca's tone remained sweet as she replied, "I'm happy to help however I can."

Her face grew animated as she talked to his *mamm*. It seemed *Mamm* had a gift for putting people at ease, and soon the two of them were chatting away. From time to time, *Mamm* included him in the conversation, but when she did, talk grew stilted. He wished they'd leave him out. He much preferred listening to Rebecca's cheerful chatter.

She turned to say something to *Mamm*, and her arm brushed his. His blood soared, but his spirits plunged as she jerked away. He'd hoped being around her again might give them a chance to mend fences, but until he could tell her the film had been destroyed for sure and certain, he'd have to deal with her coldness. Would she forgive him once she understood why he'd taken the New York job? Or had her love died completely?

When Abner pulled in front of the huge brick building with its three arched windows above the overhang, Rebecca's stomach knotted. Her first train trip. But spending time in such close proximity to Abner also made her tense. As soon as he exited the car, Rebecca exhaled the shallow breath she'd been holding. She'd make sure to sit farther away from him on the train.

They entered a large, open room, and Rebecca gawked at its high glass ceilings. Tinny, high-pitched announcements echoed around the room, bouncing off the walls, hurting her ears.

"I'll drop the bags here," Abner said, setting them beside a long wooden bench with a slatted back. "Then I'll get the tickets." He flashed his *mamm* an encouraging smile, which he turned on Rebecca, but as soon as their eyes met, it faded.

She studied the squares on the floor under her feet and tried not to mind. But she did. What was wrong with her? She'd decided to have nothing more to do with Abner, so why did it hurt so much when he kept his distance?

Rebecca seated Adah on a bench facing the ticket window, where she could stare at Abner without him noticing. After he returned with their tickets, he sat beside his *mamm*. Rather than sitting beside him, where there was more room, Rebecca squeezed in on the other side of Adah. Abner's jaw tightened, and he turned away to study the nearby crowds clustered around the doorways.

She regretted hurting his feelings, but sitting next to

him in the car had been torture enough for one day. Although the next few days would be excruciating, she'd get through it for Adah's sake.

Rebecca's ears hurt from the chattering crowds, blaring loudspeaker, and thundering trains. The announcements all sounded unintelligible to her, yet following one garbled message, Abner stood.

"That's us," he said, and herded them toward a stampeding group descending the stairs and clattering out to the platform.

Rebecca wished she could cover her ears as the train screeched into the station and shuddered to a stop. All this noise and confusion. She'd give anything to be back on the farm right now, hearing the lowing cows and cackling chickens.

Once Abner had ushered *Mamm* and Rebecca into two padded seats next to each other, he took the empty seat across the aisle. Part of him wished he were beside Rebecca, but it was also a relief to have some distance between them. Now if only he could school his thoughts and prevent himself from dwelling on her and their past.

He leaned across the aisle and set a hand on *Mamm*'s arm. "Why don't you sleep while we travel so you'll be rested for the screenings this afternoon?"

Rebecca took his cue and tucked a blanket around his *mamm*, who protested she didn't need to be swaddled like a baby. But Abner sent Rebecca an approving smile. He appreciated her caring for *Mamm*. She'd be good company for his mother during her appointments.

Rebecca's eyes sparkled, but she quickly shuttered her happy reaction. She lowered her eyelids as if to gain self-control, and when she lifted them again, her expression was blank, as if she'd wiped away all feelings for him.

A swift, sharp pain shot through him. To see their close, loving relationship turn cold was more than he could bear. Her frostiness chilled him more than the biting winter winds. Cold toes and fingers would thaw, but what about frozen hearts?

Chapter Seven

They emerged from the train into Grand Central Terminal. If Rebecca had been stunned by the Lancaster station, the cathedral-like waiting room totally overwhelmed her. The vaulted ceiling had been painted to look like constellations in the night sky. Sunlight streamed through three huge arched windows, and on each side, crystalline chandeliers sparkled between thick pillars.

Rebecca stumbled to a stop at the entrance to the cavernous room, staring in amazement. People behind her slammed into her, almost knocking her off her feet.

"I know it's beautiful," Abner said, "but we should keep moving. Most people are in a rush."

"They certainly are," Adah agreed as hurrying commuters jostled and bumped them.

Rebecca tucked the beauty of the room into her memory so she could recount it later for *Mamm* and Sarah. They'd love hearing all the details. Then she followed Abner through the room and out an exit.

She barely noticed the frigid temperature as the

odors of urine and exhaust assaulted her. All around her, horns honked and sirens blared. Towering buildings surrounded her on every side, closing in on her, blocking the pale sunshine, and throwing ominous shadows across the crowded sidewalks. Rebecca craned her neck to see the tops of the nearby skyscrapers. Her chest tightened as claustrophobia clawed at her. What if one of these tall buildings fell, crushing the scurrying people underneath the way a careless shoe squashed ants?

She started when Abner turned to her. "Could you take *Mamm*'s arm?" he asked. "If you two stay behind me, I'll try to shield you from the wind and crowds."

Tucking Adah's arm in hers, Rebecca trailed after Abner, her gaze darting from side to side to take in everything. Dirty gray slush splashed from cab and bus tires onto the sidewalk. None of the small snowbanks along the road resembled the pristine whiteness blanketing the Lancaster fields and hills.

How did people breathe when they were caged in on every side with concrete and brick? When did their ears rest from the relentless racket? How did they relax with no trees, plants, or peaceful scenery? Only a few spindly trees grew between concrete slabs. Perhaps all this busyness and grayness would chase Abner home.

But he didn't seem to share her distaste for the noise and confusion as he strode confidently down the sidewalk, sidestepping the constant stream of people heading in the opposite direction. He trailblazed a path through the crowds, protecting her and his *mamm* not only from the freezing gusts sweeping toward them, but also from being overrun by the throngs of people rushing in every direction.

Abner stopped so suddenly Rebecca almost smashed into him. She ground to a halt just before they collided and reached out to steady Adah. When Abner waved, Rebecca followed his line of vision, and her breath whooshed out in a hiss.

Paul. The shock of seeing the producer's assistant numbed her more than the arctic air. What was he doing here? The oatmeal she'd eaten earlier that morning turned into a gluey ball of sludge in her stomach, and Rebecca had the impression she was hurtling faster than the speeding train toward an impending disaster.

"I'll hail us a taxi," Paul said, "and get you out of the cold."

"Thanks." Abner was grateful to turn that responsibility over to an experienced New Yorker.

He'd forged ahead through the chaos and commotion, trying to act confident, but his insides were in turmoil. Part of him enjoyed the hustle and bustle of the city, but most of him longed to escape to the calm of the country. He'd do this job as quickly as he could so life could go back to normal. Although *Mamm*'s cancer was anything but normal, and he worried their lives might never return to its previous peacefulness.

A cab screeched to a stop, throwing a slurry of filthy snow onto the sidewalk. Rebecca jumped back to avoid getting splattered.

"It's best not to get too close to the curb in this weather," Paul said as the cabbie popped open the trunk. Paul took the suitcases from Abner, stowed them in the trunk, and slammed the lid. Then he opened the back door of the taxi and beckoned for the three of them to get inside. Abner slid partway across the seat before assisting *Mamm* into the middle. He wished he'd been able to sit beside Rebecca, but this was for the best.

Paul closed the back door and climbed into the front seat beside the driver. He gave the cabdriver directions, and the taxi bullied its way into traffic. Soon the jerking starts and stops accompanied by bleats of the horn became a syncopated rhythm, and their heads flew back and forth to the beat as the driver zipped in and out of the heavy traffic.

Abner was grateful when they glided to a stop in front of a row of shops. Paul paid the cabbie, helped Abner with the bags, and led them to a small paved courtyard beside a restaurant. Water cascaded down a carved granite wall into a reflecting pool below. To their left stood the glassed-in lobby of an elegant apartment building. As they approached, a uniformed man exited, pushing a gold-plated luggage carrier. He took the suitcases from them, placed them on the wheeled cart, and motioned for them to precede him into the building.

Paul led the way to an elevator. The man with the luggage trolley pushed it on board.

Paul placed a hand on it. "I'll take care of it from here. Thanks." He slipped some folded bills into the man's palm. "Fiftieth floor," Paul added as the elevator doors swished shut.

The operator nodded and pushed a button on an ornate panel. With an almost imperceptible hum, the elevator swished upward. As number after number lit up, Abner's stomach churned. He'd never been higher than three floors up at a mall. Fifty floors? What did they do in case of fire?

Mamm appeared uneasy as she clutched his arm, and Rebecca's cheeks were pale. Abner wished he could reach out and hold her hand. He had no idea if being in the elevator scared her or if it was Paul's nearness.

The elevator doors glided open, and Paul pushed the luggage cart out and beckoned Abner to the left. "Right this way," he said jovially. He opened a nearby door with a flourish and waved an arm for them to enter. "Here's your new home away from home."

Rebecca stepped aside to let Paul enter with the cart but stayed pressed against the wall even after he passed, and Abner wished he hadn't taken Paul up on his offer to escort them around town. But without Paul's help, he'd never be able to find his way around the city, and he needed to be sure *Mamm* made it to her appointment on time.

If being around Paul brought back bad memories for Abner, how much worse must it be for Rebecca? If only he hadn't allowed pride and desperation to blind him to the dangers of agreeing to that audition. Now she was paying the price. He deserved to be entangled in this situation, but Rebecca had been innocent.

He was only grateful she didn't know the truth about the film.

Rebecca stared around the luxurious apartment with its sleek modern furniture. How did anyone work in that tiny kitchen with no room for a table and barely any countertops? Even cooking a simple meal would be challenging. And how depressing to look out that tiny window at a brick wall and the window of another apartment that seemed close enough to touch. Rather than welcoming and homey, the living room seemed cold and impersonal. If this was where Paul lived, no wonder he and Herman had turned out so hardhearted.

Adah walked over to the windows. "We're up really high. Look how far down the street is." Her voice sounded a little shaky.

Below them, tiny cars and people streamed past. Being up this high made Rebecca a bit queasy. She tried to hide it, but Abner was studying her with an expression that indicated he understood.

"Let me show you where you'll be staying." Paul led them down a short hall and opened a door. "I assumed the ladies could share this bedroom." The room had two single beds. "I'm afraid these apartments only have one bedroom." He looked rueful. "I bet after your roomy farmhouses, these places seem small, but space is at a premium in the city."

Rebecca's stomach knotted when Paul looked at her, and she only nodded. With only one bedroom, where would Abner sleep? She hadn't thought about the possibility they'd be asked to share an apartment. Even with his *mamm* here, she'd be uncomfortable.

Paul pointed a little farther down the hall. "Thought you could stay in the adjoining apartment," he said to Abner. He unlocked the door and flung it open. This matching apartment had similar furniture, except Abner's bedroom had a king-sized bed and a view of the river in the distance.

Rebecca exhaled a long breath. At least they'd have separate apartments.

"How pretty," Adah said, but her voice was weak.

Rebecca hurried over. "You don't have to be at the clinic until two. Why don't you take a little rest now?"

"That's a great idea, *Mamm*." Abner took her arm and led her back to the other apartment.

Paul handed Rebecca three keys. "The smallest key locks this connecting door."

She fingered the small key. Not that she didn't trust Abner, but locking that door tonight would make her feel better.

"I'll get everyone's bags and take the luggage trolley back to the concierge," Paul said as he headed toward the living room. "I ordered a pizza delivery for lunch. All meals are covered while you're here. Consider it part of your pay."

From the sickish look on Abner's face, he didn't seem too keen on the job. If that was the case, why had he agreed to do it? Having room and board was helpful and convenient, but was it worth it to sacrifice your self-respect?

The minute the door closed behind Paul, Rebecca pinned him with an intense glare. "You seem uncomfortable about taking this job. Why did you take it?"

"I had my reasons." *And most of them I can't tell you.*

She leaned forward. "What are they? Because right now, all I see is someone who is leaving behind all our community's teachings, someone eager to become a TV star. What about the humility the bishop talked about last church Sunday?"

If she'd stabbed him with a knife, she couldn't have inflicted a deeper wound. He hung his head. To deny her accusation would be prideful, so Abner swallowed back his words.

He hadn't done that audition because he wanted to show off or be a star. When he did it, he needed the money to take care of *Mamm* and his brothers. He'd also wanted enough money to marry Rebecca. He'd acted on impulse, not thinking about the consequences. Most of all he regretted involving her. It had never occurred to him he could ruin her reputation. If he'd known that, he never would have done it.

And now his main reason for coming to New York was to save her reputation as well as *Mamm*'s life.

The sorrow in Rebecca's eyes troubled him, but how could he ease her distress without telling her about the film? He leaned back in the chair and shut his eyes. The heavy burden of guilt he was carrying weighed him down. Once that film had been destroyed, perhaps he and Rebecca could rebuild their relationship.

"Oh, here's your key." Rebecca handed him a gold key but held up a smaller one. "Paul gave me this to lock the door between the two apartments."

She needed to lock him out? How badly had he destroyed her trust? He hoped his hurt wasn't visible in his eyes. "Don't worry, I promise not to use the connecting door. But by all means, lock it so you'll feel safer." He couldn't keep a tinge of bitterness from his voice.

A soft knock sounded on the door, and Abner pulled it open. The pizza delivery. He set the box on the glass-topped, metal-legged dinette table.

"Did you want some?" His throat tightened. The last time they'd had pizza together had been their date before the TV disaster that broke them up. He'd picked

Rebecca up at Sarah's house, and they sneaked out together. They'd driven to Fox's Pizza in town, and they'd had so much fun laughing and talking, she'd barely made it home in time to meet her brother.

Now that she'd gotten right with the Lord, Rebecca would never agree to such trickery. Although he respected her new beliefs, he missed the old Rebecca. Did she still have fun?

Rebecca joined him at the table, her eyes suspiciously damp. Was she recalling that date too?

"Remember when—" he started to say, but she shook her head. "Look, Rebecca, we have a past together."

"A past I'd rather forget."

The lump in his throat was so huge he could barely swallow. "We can't eliminate the past, and I hope we can't erase the love we had—still have—for each other. I understand you can't trust me anymore, but can't we enjoy those memories?"

Rebecca sank into the chair at the opposite end of the table. "We don't agree on our goals for the future, so it's easier to leave all that behind and move forward with our separate lives."

She wanted locks on the separate apartments. And separate goals. Separate lives. Separate futures. But all he wanted was to be together.

Chapter Eight

Rebecca inhaled the garlicky, tomato-scented air and blinked back the moisture in her eyes. The last time she'd breathed in this scent, the two of them had shared a pepperoni pizza and a tender kiss.

Abner lifted a slice from the box, set it on one of the paper plates, and held it out to her. With trembling hands, she took the sagging plate, and the heat burned her palms. Instead of lowering his arm, Abner kept it extended as if issuing an invitation.

Across from her stood the only man she'd ever loved. If she reached out and took the hand he held out and let him draw her into his arms, they could embrace the past, let it bind them together, instead of tearing them apart.

But she'd turned her life over to God now, and they were on different paths. Rebecca lowered her eyelids to block out the temptation. She set the pizza on the table in front of her and concentrated on pulling up the strings of melting cheese sticking to the greasy paper plate.

Although she pretended interest in her task, her

whole body sensed when Abner lowered his arm and slumped into the chair. He removed another slice from the box and plopped it onto a paper plate. After the prayer, the two of them chewed in silence. Abner offered her a second piece, but she declined. Her stomach was already roiling.

While Abner ate a second slice, Rebecca cleaned up her trash and put the pizza box into the refrigerator. She fiddled with arranging the napkins on the rest of the plates and wished she had dishes to do as an excuse to stay in the kitchen.

"Did I smell food?" Adah shuffled from the bedroom. "I tried to sleep, but I'm too nervous about this afternoon."

Rebecca pulled the pizza box out again, set a slice on a plate for Adah and carried it out. "It's still warm, but I could try to heat it up for you."

"Danke," Adah said. "This will be fine."

She studied them both, her expression crestfallen. If she'd hoped this trip would allow them to work through their differences, she'd been mistaken. Rebecca had been clear about her expectations, and Abner had no desire to fulfill them.

Adah nibbled at her pizza, taking such tiny bites, Rebecca wondered if she'd only come out to play matchmaker.

By the time Paul arrived, Rebecca was relieved to end the tension in the living room. She offered him pizza, but he shook his head.

"I ate before I came. I have a taxi waiting, so we should hurry." He escorted them down in the elevator and out to the waiting cab.

Most of the ride, Rebecca and Adah sucked in breaths at near-misses as the driver steered through traffic, switching lanes and racing through yellow lights. They made it to the clinic five minutes early.

After she exited, Adah squeezed Rebecca's hand. "Will you pray for me?" she whispered.

"I have been." Between sending up prayers for protection against accidents, Rebecca had been asking God for Adah's healing. "And I'll keep on praying."

Coming up behind them, Abner winced. If only prayers had worked after *Dat*'s accident. So many people prayed for *Dat*'s healing, and none more fervently than Abner had. Other people seemed to get good results from their prayers, but with his track record, he feared praying might cause the same results. He only hoped Rebecca's prayers worked better.

The afternoon was spent on chairs, in offices, and waiting outside examining rooms, meeting with people who asked questions, took notes, pored over records, and described procedures. After hours of waiting, one of the doctors waved them into an office.

After they'd all taken seats, she said, "I'm pleased to inform you, Adah, that you've met our inclusion criteria."

Head tilted to one side, Adah stared at her with a confused look.

"That means you've been cleared to participate in the study."

"That's good, right?" Adah sounded uncertain.

The doctor nodded. "It's very good for us, if you choose to take part. This treatment has been showing promising results, so we hope it will be good for you as well."

"What happens next?" Abner asked.

"We'll explain the protocol"—she waved a hand toward the stack of papers on her desk—"the procedures, tests, possible risks, length of the study, and other details. You've heard some of this information already, but we want to be sure you are aware of everything before you sign the informed consent form."

Mamm's expression indicated she was overwhelmed, so Abner listened carefully to the explanations. He wished he'd brought a notebook to record all the information.

When the doctor noticed his frown, she stopped. "Wasn't that clear?"

"I understood it, but I've been wishing I could jot down some of the most important details."

"Your sister seems to be doing a fine job of that."

His sister?

The doctor gestured toward Rebecca. "Have you gotten most of what we've been talking about?"

She nodded. "I think so."

Abner had been so engrossed in memorizing each step of the procedure, he hadn't noticed Rebecca scribbling away. She'd planned ahead and had brought a small tablet and pen.

"We also have handouts for you to take with you, especially about the prohibited foods, expected fluid intake, chemicals to avoid, requirements for each treatment, etc." She smiled at Adah and extended that smile to Abner.

His spirits lifted. They had hope. This doctor

sounded confident that the treatment would work. Perhaps she had to be enthusiastic to sell her protocol to wary patients. He longed to believe it would cure *Mamm*.

This was more tangible than prayer. You could touch, taste, see, and hear each step being performed. You'd be able to see results. With prayers, you sent up requests that went who-knows-where. If Rebecca and *Mamm* wanted to pray, fine. But he preferred something concrete to prove healing was occurring.

Rebecca flexed her fingers as the briefing came to an end. She hoped she hadn't missed any important details. Poor Adah seemed to be struggling to stay awake, and her eyes had glazed over in the first few minutes. Rebecca doubted she'd understood even half of the information. They'd have to go over it step by step tonight.

"Do you have any questions?" The doctor glanced from one to the other.

They all shook their heads, but Rebecca suspected it was more that they were dazed. So much to take in, and in such a short time.

She passed a sheaf of papers to Adah. "These contain a simple overview of what we've just discussed. A list of rules to follow before each treatment is on top there." Then she slid the informed consent form across the desk. "We'll need your signature on this. It explains everything we went over."

Rebecca's heart went out to Abner as his *mamm* bent over the paper and scribbled her signature on the forms. His eyes sparkled with tears. Knowing that his *mamm* would be getting treatment had to be a relief for him.

She only wished he believed in the power of prayer. She bowed her head.

Dear God, please be with Adah during her treatments. Strengthen and heal her body. But help us all, especially Abner, to accept whatever Your will is in this situation. And please bring him back to You.

When she lifted her head, she met Abner's eyes. She tried to project strength and support. His eyes overflowed with thanks. They'd always been able to send messages with this special connection between them.

Adah finished signing with a flourish and set down the pen. Abner glanced at his *mamm* with affection, and then his gaze moved back to Rebecca, and the tenderness he sent her way stole her breath.

She had to remind herself of her resolve. But for right now, they were both rejoicing.

Because Adah appeared drained, they supported her out to the lobby, one on each side. Paul sat, bent over his laptop, typing away. As soon as he spotted them, he clicked something on his screen and then stood.

"How'd it go?" he asked, his gaze bouncing from one to the other. At Abner's thumbs up, he broke into a wide grin. "Awesome. Do you have a schedule yet?" he asked Adah.

But Abner answered, "The same schedule you mentioned. She'll go in on Tuesday for the treatment. Then they'll monitor her here on Wednesday and Thursday. She's free for the long weekend."

"Great, great!" He beamed at Abner. "That'll work perfectly with your work schedule. Speaking of that, are you ready to head over to the studio now to meet some of the crew?"

All the joy leaked out of Rebecca's day. The relief about Adah making it into the clinical trial paled at the thought of Abner acting on television.

His face turned gray, and his shoulders slumped. "Could we wait on that?"

Paul frowned, but then his face smoothed out. "Sure, it's been a long day for you, I understand. Herman will be disappointed, though. He was hoping to see you."

Abner rubbed his temples to ease the pounding headache that had started at the mention of Herman's name. His insides twisted at the blackmail the producer had used to get him here to New York. Even worse was the revulsion in Rebecca's eyes when Paul asked him about coming to the studio. A feeling he shared, but he had a duty to fulfill.

Squaring his shoulders, he tried to project confidence. "Why don't we plan for it first thing tomorrow?" His *mamm* had always encouraged him to do the hardest chores first and get them out of the way. And this was one of the worst he'd ever face.

"Perfect." Every one of Paul's gleaming white teeth shone in the dusk. "I'll pick you up at nine so there's less traffic to fight. Then you can get started right away."

The last thing Abner wanted to do, but the faster he completed the job, the sooner he could head home. And the sooner he could destroy that film.

Paul ushered them outside and into a waiting black limo. "This is not how I usually travel, but Herman spent the day entertaining backers for a movie premiering tomorrow night, so he needed several cars."

People had stared at their Amish clothing everywhere they went in New York. Abner was used to tourists doing that in Lancaster, so he'd taken the curious looks in stride. But seeing Amish people climbing into a limo, passersby stopped and gawked. Several took out cell phones to snap pictures. Abner shielded *Mamm* and Rebecca with his body.

After settling *Mamm* onto the luxurious seat, Abner sank into the cushiony white leather. His lips curved into a smile at Rebecca's wide eyes. She stared around, taking in the bar across from them filled with small bottles, an array of stemmed glassware, and white cloth napkins rolled into fancy shapes.

Paul opened a small door on one side, revealing refrigerator shelves. "Anyone care for a drink?"

"I don't think so," Abner said stiffly.

With a laugh, Paul pulled out some bottled waters. "You don't have any objection to these, do you?"

Abner's cheeks heated. "That would be fine. I'm sure *Mamm* is probably thirsty after all her testing."

His *mamm* had faded back against the seat and closed her eyes. She opened them slowly. Spying the water in Paul's hands, she nodded. "That would be nice. *Danke.*" Her voice was so faint, Abner worried.

Tiny frown lines appeared between Rebecca's eyebrows as she studied his *mamm*. Then she glanced at him. *Bed?* she mouthed, flicking her eyes sideways toward *Mamm*.

He nodded. *Immediately*, he mouthed back, and relief replaced the concern on her face.

The limo glided through traffic at a slower pace than the taxis, and Abner leaned back and relaxed. He partially closed his eyes but turned his head so he could focus on Rebecca, who was sitting on *Mamm*'s other side. He loved the look of wonder in her eyes as she examined the limo's interior. Not that long ago, she'd directed that gaze at him.

When they arrived at the apartment building, the elevator whisked them upstairs, and he and Rebecca helped *Mamm* into bed.

"Do you want anything to eat?" he asked her.

Mamm barely shook her head. "Not now. I'll rest first."

She sank back against the pillows and closed her eyes. The long train trip and extensive appointment had been too much. Abner regretted putting her through so much in one day. He should have brought her yesterday or he could have scheduled the appointment for tomorrow. As they shut the bedroom door behind them, Abner's phone rang.

Paul's voice boomed into the room. "Forgot to ask what you wanted for dinner. I can send up some Thai. The place near you has a great pork belly salad, and their lemongrass-jasmine rice and red coconut curry are to die for."

Mamm sometimes roasted pork belly, but he'd never had it in a salad. And the other dishes sounded interesting, but he was too tired to be adventurous tonight. Abner turned to Rebecca and raised his eyebrows.

She shrugged and mouthed, *Leftover pizza*, and he nodded.

"I think we'll just finish the pizza," he told Paul.

"You sure?"

Rebecca nodded vigorously. Evidently, she wasn't ready to try any new cuisine tonight.

"I'm sure," Abner insisted. "Thanks, though."

"Let me know if you change your mind." Paul clicked off.

Abner released a sigh. "Glad you remembered the pizza. I'm in the mood for something familiar tonight." Especially after all their new experiences. Even he, who enjoyed exploring and trying different things, would rather just relax and give his senses a rest. Although standing this close to Rebecca didn't make that easy.

She hurried into the kitchen. "I'll go warm up the pizza."

He started to say, *It's a little early for supper*, but changed his mind. Rebecca had made an excuse to avoid him. He could follow her into the tiny galley kitchen, but each time they turned around, they'd probably collide. Not that he'd mind, but he didn't want to make her any more uncomfortable than she was already.

He contented himself with standing in the doorway to watch. Judging from her expression, though, she didn't appreciate it.

The stove didn't have the usual gas burners *Mamm* had on their propane stove, but some of his *Englisch* friends had coils like those. "That looks like an electric stove," he observed. "Do you know how to cook on one?"

She pulled a cookie sheet from one of the cupboards. "I've never tried." She slid the pizza onto the metal tray and slid it into the oven. Then she examined the dials on the stovetop. "It looks pretty similar to ours at home." She pointed to the dials. "The oven is the same." She turned it on. "I assume those go to these burners. Just like my stove, this one has the little pictures that show which one is which, so that's easy to figure out."

"Makes sense." He wished he could think of something to talk about other than stoves, but standing here watching her made him breathless.

"It'll be about ten minutes." She set out two of the paper plates, then looked at him questioningly.

"Oh, I guess I'm blocking the doorway." Abner stepped aside so she could pass, and it took all his willpower not to reach out as she brushed by.

"I'll check on your *mamm* to see if she feels like eating now."

Abner wanted to point out they'd helped *Mamm* into bed only a short while ago, but he suspected Rebecca was making another excuse to avoid him. After she went into the bedroom, he sat at the table, but she took so long to reemerge, he considered going after her.

When the stove timer dinged, she popped out of the bedroom, but Abner jumped up and beat her to the kitchen. He was sliding the pizza out of the oven by the time she made it to the doorway.

"I could have gotten that."

"I know. I was trying to be helpful."

"Danke." Her *thank you* didn't sound very gracious.

He pretended not to notice her annoyance. He placed pizza on each plate and carried the hot plates toward the dinette table. Now it was her turn to back out of the way.

Rebecca glanced toward the closed bedroom door. "Your *mamm* is sound asleep, so I don't think—" She hesitated and glanced at her feet. "That is—"

"Never mind. I understand." He plopped one plate

on the table and pivoted. "I'll go to my own apartment to eat."

"I'm sorry." But her soft response seemed relieved rather than sorrowful.

As soon as he exited, the lock snicked shut. Abner wandered down the hall, unlocked the apartment door, and set his pizza on the table that matched the one he'd just left. Except this one was empty. And lonely.

Chapter Nine

Rebecca woke early the next morning, dressed, and tiptoed out to the kitchen to start breakfast. Paul had said to use anything in the cupboards or refrigerator, so she chose oatmeal. They didn't have applesauce for the oatmeal, but she found raisins and maple syrup. That would have to do.

In the drawer below the stove, she selected a pot. In the bedroom, Adah began stirring, so Rebecca set the pan on the stove and went down the hall.

"Do you need help with anything?" she asked Adah.

Abner's *mamm* shook her head. "I'll be fine."

"Did you sleep well?" Rebecca had struggled to fall asleep, surrounded by so many strange noises. Outside the window, traffic flowed by in an unending stream, unlike the silence of farm nights. The horns honking, sirens wailing, and engines roaring continued all through the night, or at least until Rebecca fell into a restless sleep near dawn.

"I had a good long rest and feel refreshed." Adah

gathered her clothes and went into the bathroom. Soon shower water drummed against the tiled walls.

Rebecca went to answer a quiet tap at the front door. Seeing Abner this early in the morning proved to be unnerving.

When she stood there without moving, Abner said, "*Gude mariye.* May I come in?"

"Oh, yes, of course." She stepped aside so he could enter. How embarrassing to be caught staring. "Your *mamm* slept well and is getting ready. I was planning to make oatmeal, but I haven't started it yet." *Stop prattling, Rebecca.* Trying to cover up her embarrassment with a flow of words only made her appear more foolish. "Anyway," she said, "I'll go into the kitchen to make breakfast."

"That sounds good."

The smile Abner sent her way made her shaky legs even more wobbly. She turned abruptly and almost collided with the archway to the kitchen. Stopping herself just in time, she held out a hand to steady herself.

"Are you all right?" Abner asked.

"I'm fine." Rebecca regretted her snappish voice. "I'm just not used to the apartment layout. Or how close together everything is." Or how close together she and Abner were.

Breathe, she commanded herself. Taking a few deep breaths to calm her racing heart, she hurried into the kitchen, eager to put some distance between her and Abner.

He pivoted so he could stand in the kitchen doorway, making Rebecca even more nervous than she already was. She forced herself to move slowly and calmly despite the jitters inside.

By the time she'd found the kitchen equipment she needed and measured out the milk and oatmeal, Adah had emerged from the bedroom. She joined Abner in the doorway.

Setting the oatmeal pot on the coils, she turned the burner to medium. No flames appeared. She fiddled with the dial, and the coils turned red.

"I think with electric stoves, you have to wait a while for those coils to heat the food," Abner said. "Some of my *Englisch* friends have stoves like this."

Rebecca's cheeks burned. He must have thought her a fool when she bent to look for flames, especially since they'd talked yesterday about the stove being electric. She turned the heat back to medium again. When oatmeal started to sputter, she grabbed the wooden spoon to stir it. The liquid boiled up into bubbles that popped on the surface. Time to turn the heat down. She turned it to low, but instead of cooling down, the oatmeal boiled faster, sticking to the bottom of the pot. The surface turned into a mass of huge bubbles exploding like mini-volcanoes and splattering the stove. She snapped the burner off, but the oatmeal boiled up and over the sides of the pot, puddling on the stove.

Abner rushed over and lifted the pot from the burner as oatmeal kept cascading down the sides, splashing onto the burner with loud hisses. "Electric burners hold their heat, so even when you turn them off, they still stay hot. It's not like propane."

Rebecca blinked rapidly to hold back tears.

Both Abner and Adah would think she didn't know

how to cook. "I—I've never used an electric stove, so I guess I made some mistakes."

"You can't expect to get it right on the first try." Adah's soothing voice calmed Rebecca a little. "I'm sure we can eat some of this. It isn't the first time we've had a kitchen disaster." Adah's comical expression made Rebecca giggle.

Maybe they could still salvage the meal.

The pot handle bit into Abner's palm as he gripped it tightly. Rebecca's closeness and her bell-like laugh made breathing impossible. A sharp intake of air burst from his lips. He hoped the others would mistake it for laughter.

Maneuvering around Rebecca, he carried the still-dripping pot to the sink. He kept his hands underneath to catch as many blobs as possible, but some dotted the kitchen floor. He set the pan in the sink. In the narrow kitchen, she was so near he could reach out and pull her into his arms. And she'd been staring at him. The rosy flush creeping up her cheeks gave it away. She immediately looked away.

"I—I'll get the bowls." She reached behind her on the counter and handed him blue pottery bowls.

He almost dropped them as his fingers brushed hers. She kept her eyes downcast, but surely that jolt affected her too. And she still hadn't let go of the bowls.

As if realizing her mistake, she jerked her hands back. "I'll get the spoons. They don't have any apple-sauce, but I thought maple syrup and raisins…"

"That'll do," *Mamm* said behind her, startling both of them.

Rebecca turned away, leaving him bereft. The kitchen seemed emptier when she exited to set the spoons on the dinette table. He spun back to the sink and glopped a large spoonful of the gluey oatmeal into each bowl.

"I don't know if there's a trick to stopping the heat when you're done. Turning the burner off doesn't work. I guess lifting the pot off is best."

"I'd rather have a flame I could control." *Mamm* opened a few drawers. "I found the spoons."

Abner needed a buffer between him and Rebecca. He'd never had breakfast with her, and doing so seemed so intimate. Like something they'd do together when they were married. Yet he couldn't make himself leave the kitchen. "I'll wait in case you need any help."

From the look she shot him, she'd seen through his flimsy excuse. "I think I can manage now."

He seized on another excuse. "I'll just clean up the floor while I wait." Wetting a cloth, he squatted and wiped up all spots. "Be careful you don't slip," he warned *Mamm*. But she wasn't the only one who needed to proceed with caution.

Grateful to escape from the kitchen, Rebecca set spoons on the table. She had to find a way to keep her distance from Abner. Every time she was around him, she ended up fighting her attraction to him. She never should have come to New York.

After they sat down for breakfast, with Abner across from her, they all prayed and then lifted their heads at the same time. Rebecca kept her attention on her bowl. The oatmeal had a slight charcoal taste.

A banging on the door signaled Paul had arrived. Abner hopped up to let him in.

"I didn't realize you'd be here so early, or we would have made breakfast for you too."

"No time. I already grabbed a Danish." He held out a bakery box. "I brought some for your breakfast too." After setting the box on the table, he turned to Abner. "We need to go. Herman wants to make up for not having you at the studio yesterday."

Paul's phone buzzed, and he glanced at the screen. "I'll just step into the hallway to answer this. Please hurry."

Rebecca's breakfast curdled in her stomach. As soon as the door shut behind Paul she said, "Abner, please don't do this."

"I have to." He met her gaze, a plea for understanding in his eyes.

"No, you don't. The church could help. You can get another job." Her words tumbled out, desperate, begging.

"I'm sorry, Rebecca, but I promised." Abner scraped out his bowl, bowed his head briefly, then jumped up from the table and followed Paul out the door.

Just before the door slammed, Paul called out, "I've ordered two subs for your lunch. They'll deliver them at noon. And no tip needed. Forgot to tell you that yesterday."

The door swung shut with a bang.

Rebecca pinched her lips together, and her spoon clattered into her bowl. The cloying stickiness of the maple syrup still clung to her tongue, but the bile rising from her stomach threatened to burn its sweetness away. She swallowed hard and turned to Adah. "I'm sorry I failed to convince him to stay. You said I had influence over him, but that doesn't seem to be the case."

Adah reached over and patted her hand. "You have more influence than you realize, but with Paul here, he couldn't back out on his agreement."

He could, but he wouldn't.

"I'm worried coming to New York made it seem like I agreed with his decision."

"I'm sorry. I never should have asked you to do this."

"*Ach*, Adah, no. I'm happy to be here for your sake. It's just that…" Rebecca couldn't finish her sentence because no matter what she said, it would seem as if she was criticizing Abner's *mamm*. And that's the last thing she wanted to do.

"I've been both a burden and an excuse. Abner felt he had to bring me to New York. We never even looked into other possibilities. Perhaps some hospitals in Pennsylvania had clinical trials."

They'd rather pressured Adah into coming here. Rebecca had backed Abner on it, but now she wished she hadn't. The clinical trials sounded promising, and if they worked, it would be worth it. But not if they lost Abner.

Rebecca's eyes haunted Abner the whole time they traveled to the studio. All he wanted to do was turn to Paul and say, *I can't do this*. Several times his lips formed the words, but they never came out of his mouth.

The desire to flee increased when they pulled up outside a long brick building with a studio name emblazoned on it. Why had he agreed to come? Only the thought of the film in Herman's possession kept him following Paul into the multi-storied building's lobby, where Paul showed a pass and Abner signed in and received a nametag labeled *Visitor*.

When they exited the elevator, Paul led the way down a long corridor and tapped at a door. A gruff *Come in* came through the door. Paul opened the door and, putting an arm around Abner's shoulders, led him to the side of a room filled with cameras and people sitting on chairs.

"It's about time," Herman barked. "I thought I told you to have him here early."

Paul shrugged. "Traffic."

"Okay, everyone." Herman moved to the low stage at the front of the room. "Here's the moment we've all been waiting for." He gestured toward Abner. Paul nudged him to toward the spot where Herman stood.

Abner drew back. "I agreed to do this, but not with cameras."

"They aren't shooting right now. They'll wait for a signal."

"No." Abner stood firm. "You tricked me into doing this once before."

Herman snorted. "Tricked you? I don't think so. You were eager to get in front of the camera. The only one who was tricked was your girlfriend. And we didn't do that tricking."

Abner froze in place. Herman was absolutely right. Paul had asked Abner to do a screen test with Rebecca. The producers wanted a dance scene inside the barn and a kissing scene in the courting buggy outside. He'd agreed to be filmed, and he'd done what they'd asked.

The only one who didn't know about the filming was Rebecca. He'd been afraid she'd object. And he'd been right. After she found out, she broke up with him.

"Okay, okay, you win." Herman waved to the camera people. "Step back from the cameras."

Huh? Who won what? Abner puzzled over it as the camera operators moved back or sat on chairs. Then it dawned on him. While he stood there thinking, Herman assumed he was standing his ground and refusing to go up front until he was certain he wouldn't be filmed. His guilty conscience had stopped him in his tracks, but it had ended the standoff with Herman.

"What are you waiting for now?" Herman groused. "Nobody's filming you. Get on up here so we can get started."

Abner disliked heading to the stage with all eyes on him. It definitely had turned out for the best that he hadn't signed that contract to act on the show. He wouldn't have liked acting in front of an audience. This would be his penance. For everything he'd done and for hurting Rebecca.

After he climbed onto the stage, Herman made him rotate so the audience could see his front, his side, his back, and his other side. Abner stood self-consciously in each position, conscious of every person in the room scrutinizing him. It was nerve-racking.

"You're way too stiff," Herman snapped. "Loosen up."

His command only made Abner tighten up more.

"Oh, for—" He stopped, and Paul burst out laughing.

"Why don't you try, 'Oh, for Pete's sake'?" he suggested, and Herman scowled.

Paul turned to the audience to explain. "When we were in Lancaster, an elderly Amish woman threatened to wash his mouth out with lye soap if he swore. Now he stops before he curses or takes the Lord's name in vain." He laughed, but then sobered. "I shouldn't make fun of him, or her. She helped to turn my life around."

"Yeah, now he refuses to work on Sundays and goes off to church instead." Herman's words dripped with sarcasm. "And he won't go out drinking with me after work anymore."

"Don't worry," Paul said, "We'll soon have you reading the Bible."

A few people in the audience snickered.

"I wouldn't count on that," Herman growled. "And stop sidetracking this with your crazy religious stuff." He glanced at Abner. "No offense."

Paul chuckled, and Herman glared at him.

Abner shifted from one foot to the other. Standing up here, doing nothing, while they argued made him antsy. And the spotlights shone down, generating so much heat that his brow beaded with sweat.

"Look, you need to relax," Herman said. "Tell you what. Why don't you playact a little?"

Abner stared at him suspiciously and then checked the cameras. He wouldn't put it past Herman to tape him on the sly.

"Don't worry," Paul called out. "I'll keep an eye on the camera crew. I promise nobody will film you."

Abner nodded but remained uncertain whether or not Paul could be trusted. He'd been the more ethical of the two men, but they'd both pulled off a big scam.

He turned to Herman. "What do you want me to do?"

"What do you usually do at home in the mornings?"

"You mean like milking the cows and doing the farm chores?"

A ripple of laughter rolled through the actors in the audience.

"Yeah, sure." Herman glanced around. "You need any props?"

"If I'm milking, a stool would help."

"Since it's an imaginary cow, I assume you can use an imaginary bucket."

One of the girls in the audience giggled.

"Right," Abner agreed. "I promise not to get too much milk on the floor."

Herman smiled. "Good, good. You're getting into it." He waved a hand toward a stool behind one of the cameras. "Would that do?"

"It's a little high, but I can pretend the cow's on a platform."

"You good at pretending?"

Abner nodded. He'd done a lot of pretending over the years. Pretending to listen when he was daydreaming. Pretending to be brave when he was scared. Pretending to be strong when *Dat* died so *Mamm* and his brothers would have someone to lean on.

The stool clattered down next to him, startling him from the past.

"You have a very expressive face," Herman said. "With that and an ability to pretend, you'd make a great actor."

Except Abner had just learned he had stage fright. And he'd never be able to face Rebecca. Those were enough of a deterrent. So was the film Herman was using to blackmail him.

"Okay, I'll step out of the way here, and you can do your chores. No need to talk unless you need to explain something."

Herman's eyebrows rose when Abner walked all the way to the other side of the stage.

"I have to walk out to the barn," Abner explained. "I don't live there."

Appreciative chuckles came from the audience.

"Makes sense." Herman waved a hand. "Go ahead, get started."

Abner mimed opening the kitchen door and striding out to the barn. He made a creaking noise when he opened the barn door. That made it seem more realistic. He went down the line, feeding each horse and cow some hay and then giving them all water. He did a few chores while he waited for the animals to finish eating. Then he got the first cow ready for milking.

As he sat on the stool, pretending to milk a cow, the stage disappeared, and he was home in the barn. The scent of hay, manure, and warm cow filled his nostrils. Bossie's tail twitched impatiently, but he kept milking.

"Okay, we don't need to see ten minutes of the same motion." Herman's voice jerked Abner back to the studio.

"But I haven't even finished one cow. I have three more to do."

"I think you're sufficiently warmed up. We won't need to see you milk all those cows. Do you feel more relaxed now?"

Abner had to admit he did. While he'd been milking,

he'd forgotten all about the audience and submerged himself in the action. "Yes."

"Good. Why don't you do that walk from the house to the barn again?" This time Herman waited for him at the imaginary barn door. "Notice the set of the shoulders." Waving his hand just above Abner's shoulders, he turned to the audience.

Heads nodded.

Herman motioned for Abner to turn his back. "Now sideways," he commanded.

Abner pivoted.

"Can you see the humility in his stance? Most of you are swaggering around with conceited attitudes." Herman whirled his finger in a circle, which Abner suspected meant he was to rotate again.

"But not only humility. See how he stands straight and tall, denoting a strength of character and a different kind of pride. The pride of integrity."

Abner made a choking sound, and Herman glared at him. He hadn't intended to be used as an example of godly living. He couldn't claim that pride of integrity. "I'm not—"

Herman waved a hand to silence him. "If you're not," he said in a low voice so the audience couldn't overhear, "pretend you are."

Abner could pretend to milk a cow or open a barn door, but when it came to ethics, he couldn't pretend. Maybe life would be easier if he could. He could go to the hymn sings and social activities, be part of the group. He could pretend he had no doubts about his faith and God. He could pretend to believe and join the church, so he could marry Rebecca. But his conscience wouldn't let him lie.

After Abner left, Rebecca scrubbed the stove top and cleaned up the dishes. As she held the handle to scour the oatmeal pot, she relived Abner brushing against her to grab the erupting pan. If only they had both joined the church...

"What can I do to help?" Adah's question made Rebecca jump.

She'd been lost in daydreams of how life could have been, but it wasn't reality. And she hadn't answered Adah. "Nothing left to do but clean this pot. I'm almost done."

"I'm not used to being idle. Once you're done, I could mop the kitchen floor. All the rest of the floors have carpet, and they're spotless."

"I planned to do the floor as soon as I'm done here. It won't take long. This room is so small."

"Yes, I don't imagine they do much cooking in here."

Rebecca nodded. "I expect you're right. Paul eats out a lot. Maybe the people who live in places like this do that."

And with only one or two people in these apartments, they must be lonely too.

Chapter Ten

Abner spent the rest of the morning walking across the stage, followed by all the male actors who were copying him. The afternoon was spent talking to different actors so they could copy his accent. Abner winced at the attempts to imitate his speech.

As the day drew to a close, one question burned in Abner's mind, but who could he ask? He glanced around the room, trying to find a friendly face. Someone from the camera crew might know the answer.

He waited until Herman was in the midst of berating one of the actors and slipped over to a cameraman who'd smiled at him a few times. "Hello."

"Hey, how ya doin'?" The man greeted him with a grin. "You really milk cows every morning?"

"Yes, at five so I can get to work on time."

"Ugh, five?" When Abner nodded, he shook his head. "Better you than me, just saying."

Should he continue the conversation a little longer or go straight to his question? He asked one more question out of politeness. "So, what's it like being behind a camera?"

"Here, see for yourself." The man swung the camera toward him and pointed to the viewfinder. When Abner hesitated, he said, "Go ahead. Take a peek."

Abner did as he suggested. Everything looked smaller than in real life.

"Swing it around a bit." The man panned the camera along the stage and stopped at Herman. He adjusted something, and Herman's face ballooned until his screaming mouth filled the space. Every tooth and even his tongue was visible. Abner stepped back. That was too intense. And he didn't feel right invading Herman's privacy. The image likely would give him nightmares.

"You can move it around to see other things. Like this."

Abner shook his head. "That's all right. I'd rather not." He'd gotten sidetracked from his main purpose. "Is it true you Amish don't believe in photographs? That's what Paul told us anyway."

"Yes, we don't want to be photographed."

"How come, man? I've never met anyone who didn't want to get in front of the camera. Most of the time we have trouble with camera hogs."

Abner tried to explain. "The Bible says not to make graven images, so we try to follow what God says."

The man looked incredulous. "You do everything the Bible tells you to?"

Abner hadn't expected to give a sermon in a TV studio. But the cameraman's question deserved an answer. "We're supposed to," Abner said, "but I often fall short."

The man laughed and clapped him on the back. "Glad to hear you're human."

Abner shook his head. That response sounded as if the cameraman approved of sinning. And now the cameraman's question would haunt him the rest of the day.

He'd been planning to find the recording of him and Rebecca, and he hoped to find a way to destroy it. But that question about doing everything the Bible said convicted him. Although Herman had broken his promise, the tape still belonged to him, so Abner had no right to take it—that would be stealing. Maybe if he located it, though, he could ask Paul for permission. Somehow, he doubted Herman would keep his promise.

The cameraman stood and stretched. Abner had to ask him now before he left.

He tried to act casual. "So where do you store all the old tapes or films? You must have a lot of them."

"Sure do. Super old ones would be kept in the archives. The more recent ones would be in the library." The man studied him. "Why? You interested?"

Extremely. But he kept his tone noncommittal. "Yeah."

"I could show you if you want."

This had been easier than Abner had expected. Paul was huddled with a young girl, pointing out things in the booklet she had in her hand. Herman was still berating the young man he'd been yelling at earlier.

"Sure," he agreed. "It'll keep me occupied until Paul's ready to go." His heart thumped painfully in his chest as he accompanied the cameraman through the door and down the hallway.

"I'm Zander, by the way." He stuck out his hand. "Sorry, should have introduced myself earlier."

Shaking Zander's extended hand, Abner said, "Nice to meet you." *Very nice. And possibly lifesaving.* "I'm Abner."

Zander laughed. "I know. Herman invokes your name a million times a day."

Abner stopped abruptly and frowned. "He does?"

"Don't worry. It's all good." Zander motioned for Abner to come along. "You're the role model. He's always saying, 'When Abner did this...' Or 'Once Abner gets here, you'll see how atrocious your accent is.' Stuff like that."

"I see." Abner cringed to think he was being held up as a role model. Not only because *Mamm* had tried to instill humility in him from the time he was a toddler, but also because his recent behavior had been far from exemplary.

"Everyone's been waiting for you to arrive to show us the error of our ways." Zander chuckled.

"I'm not sure I'm the right one for that." Even hearing that made him sick to his stomach.

Zander clapped him on the back. "Don't be modest, man." He waved a hand to indicate Abner's clothes and black hat. "Anyone brave enough to wear that get-up in public must have some, um"—he fumbled for the right word—"strength of character." Then he mumbled under his breath, "I see why Herman's all tied up in knots. Finding substitutes for profanities isn't easy."

Abner squirmed. Being praised was uncomfortable. But knowing how unworthy he was of praise made it even worse. He only wore the clothes out of habit, not

out of duty to God. Or did he? Deep inside, despite all
his rebellion against the Lord, part of him still retained
the reverence for God's Word and His call to be separate from the world.

They took an elevator down to a lower level. Abner
noted the G that Zander pushed. He might need to do
this himself. If the room had a lot of tapes, it could take
him several trips to find the right one. Perhaps he could
slip out whenever Herman called for a lunchbreak like
he had today.

Zander opened one of the double doors, and they
went through another set of glass doors. "It's temperature and humidity controlled in here. Don't know about
you, but my throat gets parched when I'm in here. No
food or drinks allowed."

Inside the entrance, Abner stopped short, and his
stomach sank. The multi-storied room had a metal spi-
ral staircase winding up to the two floors overhead. All
around him shelves stretched from the floor until they
touched the ceiling under the second-floor walkway.
The second and third floors were designed the same
way. And on the first floor, row after row of wooden
library shelving lined the center of the room. Each shelf
was stuffed full of books, papers, file folders, tapes,
thin boxes.

"Can I help you find anything?" a creaky old voice
asked.

Abner jumped and turned in the direction of the
sound. He hadn't noticed the elderly man sitting at a
desk just inside the door. But it would make sense that
all this material would be guarded.

"We're just looking," Zander said, but then turned to Abner. "Unless there's something specific you wanted?"

There certainly was, but Abner wasn't about to share his quest. "That's all right." He almost followed Zander to the stacks, then thought better of it. If he did this himself, it would take years. Surely the librarian could at least point him to the right section. Then he'd do his own searching.

"Actually," he said to the librarian, "could you tell me how everything is arranged? For example, where would I find the most recent movies?"

The librarian seemed pleased to have a question to answer. He cleared his throat. "Telling you about the collection could take all day."

Abner hated to douse the eager light in his eyes, but he didn't have all day. "I need to go soon." At the man's disappointed expression, he hastened to add, "But I'll come back again when I have more time."

The man's hopeful look added to Abner's guilt. When he came back, he didn't intend to do anything but look for the film. He'd basically just told a lie, despite the fact that his statement was true. He should clarify the truth. "That is, I—"

The librarian held up a hand. "It's all right. I totally understand. Everyone's so busy these days, they don't even have time for the common courtesies."

Abner tried to remember if he'd extended a greeting to the man or even asked his question politely. He suspected the answer was *no.* "I'm sorry."

"Don't be. I know you young ones are so busy. Not like me. I have plenty of lonely hours to fill."

Abner's heart went out to the man. He himself had

experienced that same loneliness last night, but he didn't want to make a promise he might not keep.

Zander had strolled over to some nearby shelves. The two of them needed to go soon before Paul started wondering where he was.

The librarian scraped back his chair and stood. "Down here we have the classics. All the items that are used regularly. Lesser-known material is stored on the two upper floors. That section of the third floor has brief clips and—"

"Where would the most recent ones of those be?"

"Everything's filed alphabetically by producer, then by date."

"Thanks, I'll just take a quick peek up there." That should be easy. Find Herman's name and the most recent dates. He started up the stairs with hope blossoming in his heart.

Five minutes later, he'd hit rock bottom. He'd found Herman's name, but only a few early dates. In fact, everywhere he looked, the latest dates seemed to be from the 1990s, with a few from the very early 2000s scattered in.

"Hey, Abner," Zander called up, "I need to go. My girlfriend's expecting me to meet her for dinner. Gotta catch a subway soon."

Abner clattered down the stairs. "I was checking Herman's shelves up there, and he only has a few tapes from the late 1990s."

"That'd be about right."

"Then which section here holds the films for the TV shows they've shot like last week or last month?"

"Whadda ya mean?"

"You know, don't they have video tapes and stuff?" Abner hoped he sounded sophisticated and knowledgeable, but Zander laughed.

"You looking for DVDs? Those didn't start coming out until the late 1990s. If you're interested in those, I'd suggest Herman's office. He has quite a collection— everything he's ever done, plus lots of stuff by other producers and directors."

"Yes, that's what I'm interested in."

But Zander was preoccupied checking his watch. "Gotta go. Can you find your own way back to Paul?"

Abner nodded. Good thing he'd paid attention coming down here. "See you tomorrow."

"Later, man." Zander flapped his hand and took off running.

Abner had no trouble getting back to the room and was relieved to see Paul still engrossed in a discussion. Herman had moved on to harangue someone else.

If the film he was trying to locate was in Herman's office, how would he find out where the office was? And once he did, how long would it take to locate the film?

After Rebecca finished cleaning the kitchen, she headed into the living room to find Adah huddled in the chair, staring out the window, her face settled into lines of deep sorrow.

"Are you all right?" Rebecca asked.

"What?" Abner's *mamm* turned startled eyes in Rebecca's direction.

"You look so sad."

Adah shook her head as if to dislodge her gloomy

thoughts and pasted on a smile that didn't quite reach her eyes. "I should be grateful for the free treatments and staying in this"—she waved her hand around, indicating the room around them—"lovely apartment and for Abner earning money."

She paused, and Rebecca waited for her to continue. When she did, her voice quavered. "I'm not happy with what Abner's doing, and I want to see him come back to God."

Rebecca settled beside Adah on the couch and set a hand on her arm. Abner's *mamm* had always supported them when they broke the rules, or maybe she'd just been too overwhelmed to discipline a rebellious son. Or giving him freedom may have been her way of supporting him through his *dat*'s death. Perhaps she'd been afraid to lose him after she'd just lost her husband.

"I let him be wild during *Rumschpringa* because I thought he'd soon see the error of his ways." Adah's voice cracked. "His *dat* was wild as a *youngie*. They both have—or had—adventurous spirits that are difficult to tame."

"I know." His spirit was what first attracted Rebecca to Abner. She, too, had an adventurous streak that had caused her to rebel, but unlike Adah, her parents and Jakob had tried hard to curb it. Perhaps if they'd given her more freedom, it would have prevented her defiance.

Adah sighed. "Making decisions as a parent is never easy. I always second-guess my choices. Right now, I'm wondering if I made the wrong decision in coming here."

"Of course you didn't," Rebecca hastened to assure

her. "Taking care of your health is important to your family."

At the word *family*, Adah's eyes filled with tears. "But what about the boys? They must be so frightened. First they lose their *dat*, and now this."

"We'll be leaving for home the day after tomorrow, so you'll see them soon."

"I'm not sure I can go through with this. They did say I'm free to drop out anytime. It would be better for them if I quit before I start the treatments." She focused on the heavy gray storm clouds amassing over the skyscrapers. "I don't know if I can face months of coming here and leaving the boys behind."

"Then think how upset they'd feel if they lost you. Being in this clinical trial means you have a good chance at preventing that."

"I suppose that's true, but right now, I feel so guilty being away from them." A few tears trickled down her cheeks. "And I miss them so much. We've never been separated before, so they don't understand."

Rebecca's heart went out to her, and to the boys. She couldn't imagine being a child and losing your *dat* and then having your mom gone for most of the week. "Could they come along with us next week? Maybe seeing where you're staying and what's happening would help them."

Adah's face brightened, but then fell. "As much as I'd love that, I can't pull the three older ones out of school. And I wouldn't feel right bringing Philip by himself."

"I'm sure Sarah would allow them to take time off under the circumstances. In fact, she could give me their lessons. If the school board approves, I'd be happy to teach them when I'm not with you at the clinic."

"Oh, Rebecca, that would be wonderful."

Rebecca's mood rose temporarily with Adah's, but she'd been planning to use teaching as an excuse for not returning next week. She was hoping to find someone else to take her place. Now, unless the school board objected, she'd tied herself into coming back another week. A thought that made her both elated and nervous.

During the next day's lunch break, Abner approached Zander. "You mentioned the more recent DVDs might be in Herman's office. I'd love to check them out if that's possible." Today would be his last chance to check for the film before they left for home early tomorrow morning.

"I'd planned to grab a sandwich and then try some new camera angles, but if it's important to you, I suppose the experimenting can wait."

"*Dank*—I mean, thank you."

"Sure, man, no prob."

Abner trailed Zander to the food table and pointed at the rows of fat green and orange cylinders. "What kind are these?"

"The wraps, you mean?" He pointed to the green one. "The spinach wrap is a veggie sandwich. The other's a tomato tortilla with crab salad filling."

Zander took one of each; Abner did the same. Then he speared a huge dill pickle from a barrel. Zander grabbed a small handful of blue corn chips. Abner settled for a serving of potato chips.

They carried their plates and munched their wraps

as Zander led him along the corridor. Both sandwiches were tasty, so Abner was glad he'd taken two. He polished off the pickle and chips before they reached a fancy wooden door with a gold nameplate.

If Abner had to return more than once, this would be easy to find.

Zander reached for the doorknob. "He usually keeps it locked, so you might have to ask for the key."

Abner couldn't do that. Herman would know immediately what Abner was looking for, and he'd hide it.

"We're in luck," Zander said. The knob turned, and he opened the door.

Once again Abner was faced with shelves jam-packed with booklets, videos, file folders, thin boxes, and DVDs. How would he ever find what he needed? He had to look now because who knows when he'd find the office open again.

"Is Herman's stuff in any special place?"

"You bet it is. That huge wall of floor-to-ceiling shelves is all his. The two smaller bookcases along each wall are people he admires."

Abner didn't say aloud what he was thinking. *It seems he admires himself a whole lot more.* He strode over to the shelves and checked the dates. They seemed to run across the rows and from top to bottom, so the newest material would be more accessible. *Good.*

"Thanks." Abner squatted and ran his finger along the lowest row to this year. Some of the spines had been marked with dates. Abner moved to the fall. He pulled each one out individually to read the titles.

He had no idea what he'd do once he found it. He shouldn't take it out of the office, because that would be stealing. Would he be able to convince Herman—or maybe Paul—to give it to him?

And would he even know it if he saw it? He hoped it would be dated. Many of the spines were. The tape would probably be marked "Amish." At least he hoped so. But none of the tapes had a label like that. And almost everything he pulled out indicated it was a script, DVD, or Blu-ray.

"Where would Herman keep copies of screen tests or shows he's working on?"

"You won't find anything like that here, man. All our storage is on the cloud."

The cloud? Abner glanced up toward the ceiling, but then his cheeks heated. Obviously, Zander didn't mean real clouds.

Evidently, sensing his confusion, Zander said, "The cloud's a special storage area on computers. It allows you to keep large files. Very handy for this type of work."

So Herman had the film on his computer? Now what? How could Abner ever gain access to that?

Chapter Eleven

As the train steamed away from the city early Friday morning, Rebecca's disappointment surprised her. She'd gotten used to the city sounds, and although she still didn't like the noise, most of the time it faded into the background. But if she were honest, she wouldn't miss the city as much as she'd miss being around Abner.

Seeing him every day and eating meals together was both heavenly and painful. After two years of stolen time, sneaking out to be together, worrying all the time she'd be caught and her family would find out, they now had time together with no one to spy on them or criticize their behavior. Except now she'd repented and intended to live her life for God, so they were further apart than ever.

But what about Abner? His *mamm* obviously regretted letting him stray so far from the faith. And now that he'd had a taste of acting and city life, was it too late? Would he ever return? He'd told her he'd take baptismal classes in the spring, but would this experience change his mind?

She leaned around a sleeping Adah to question him. "How was the acting?" She tried not to let her distaste slip into her words.

"So far I've mostly done miming." Abner smiled. "My cow-milking demo seemed to be a hit."

"You're teaching them to milk cows? They have cows in the city?"

Abner's laughter drifted around her, and she wrapped her arms around herself to ward off the ache. How she'd always loved that sound!

"Maybe I should bring a real cow in to demonstrate. That'd shake things up a bit."

"I'm sure it would."

"If only I could. Can you picture Herman's shock? His scowl?"

Rebecca giggled. "Well, it would be funny except I'd feel sorry for the poor cow."

"Me too."

Abner slid over the window seat and patted the aisle seat beside him. "Why don't you sit over here to talk so we don't disturb *Mamm*?"

"I don't think—" At his crestfallen expression, she reconsidered. They were on a train, after all. What harm could there be in talking? Well, except for struggling with his magnetic pull. "All right."

She stood and stepped over Adah's legs. The train swayed, and she almost tumbled into Abner's lap. He grasped her arms to steady her, and they gazed into each other's eyes. All the old heat blazed between them. Her arms tingled from his touch. Coming over here had been too dangerous. Rebecca needed to flee.

Before she could act on her one rational idea, Abner,

holding on to one of her arms, steered her gently into the seat. As soon as she was seated, she withdrew her arm and tucked it close to her side so she didn't accidentally brush against his sleeve.

Hurt flickered in his eyes but was rapidly replaced by resignation.

Sitting this close to him, Rebecca struggled to remember what they'd been talking about. *Oh, yes, cows.* She seized on that as a safe conversation. "What did you mean about milking cows?"

"Herman suggested I pretend to go through my morning routine, so I sat on a stool and milked a pretend cow."

Rebecca giggled. "I would have liked to see that."

"You would?" The longing look he gave her told her they were wandering into hazardous territory.

"Yes, I'm sure it was humorous," she said firmly, hoping he'd get the message.

The conversation had been going so well. Why had he ruined it by making his feelings so obvious? He fumbled for a way to get things back to their original friendly footing. "Well, I left my poor cow partially unmilked because they were too impatient to sit through the whole process."

"I suppose imaginary cows probably don't work well on TV." Her chilly tone put even more distance between them.

"This wasn't on TV. I made sure of that before I started. I refused to be filmed."

"You did? How did Herman feel about that?"

"He wasn't happy, but he agreed to my terms. If he hadn't, I wouldn't have gone."

She turned to him, an incredulous look on her face. "You told them they couldn't film you?"

Abner nodded. "I promised you I wouldn't ever be in a film. I tore up that contract for the TV show. You saw me do it. I've kept my promise."

"Why didn't you tell me?"

"I started to, but we got sidetracked." He'd had plenty of opportunities to tell her since then, but he'd avoided mentioning the studio because he didn't want to face her frowns.

Rebecca studied him as if gauging his truthfulness. "I wish I'd known."

"What difference does it make?" He couldn't stop some frustration from seeping into his words.

"I would have worried less, and so would your *mamm*." She turned puzzled eyes in his direction. "But if you're not acting in a film, what are you doing at the studio?"

"Helping the actors act more Amish."

She winced.

His saying it aloud made it sound awful. And maybe it was. He hadn't thought about it before, but wasn't there something inherently wrong about teaching people to fake your religion?

Being Amish wasn't about walking and talking a certain way or wearing modest clothing. It wasn't the outer appearance. Being Amish was a lifestyle, a heart choice and daily actions. He'd conveyed none of that to the actors. He was creating a façade, a hollow empty shell with no substance inside. He was doing a disservice to the actors, but how could he demonstrate the truth about the Amish commitment to God, to the church, and to the community when he himself was living a lie?

"I don't know how I feel about actors pretending they're Amish."

"I hadn't thought about it before I told you, but now I see I never should have agreed." He'd have to finish out his contract, but his next lessons would be more authentic. He wasn't sure Herman would like his presentations, though. Maybe he'd even fire him.

Although Rebecca was grateful to have the weekend at home, she found herself longing to be back in New York. Rebecca met with Sarah to plan the boys' lessons, and she packed lesson plans and a guide to New York City she'd borrowed from the library. But a few hours into their Monday morning train trip, she and the other adults were having trouble containing four lively boys who were bouncing from seat to seat.

"Look at that," Philip exclaimed, pointing out the window.

His brothers all rushed over, elbowing each other out of the way to see.

"Ouch!" Peter cried. "I was here first. *Mamm*, make James move over to let me see."

Esther caught Rebecca's eye, and she nodded. They each corralled one boy and set him by a window seat before taking the aisle seats next to him. The boys had begged to sit together, but following their lead, Abner took James by the hand and settled John, the quietest of the four, beside his *mamm*.

When the train pulled into the station, Esther sucked in a breath. "It's so huge. What if we get separated?"

"When we were small and went into one of the bigger stores in town," Rebecca said, "*Mamm* always told us, if we got lost, we should sit by the exit. Then she'd know where to look for us."

"That's a great idea," Abner said. "Did you hear that, boys?"

His brothers all nodded.

It was a helpful strategy, but Rebecca didn't want to leave things to chance. "If we each take the hand of the boy sitting next to us, we can make sure no one gets lost."

"Oh, thank you," Esther said. "I was worried about keeping an eye on all four of them at once in such a big building." Her eyes wide, she stared out the window at all the people. "It all seems so…"

"Overwhelming," Rebecca supplied. "At least that's how I felt last week when I arrived." After one trip, she was still impressed with the building but felt more like a seasoned traveler.

"Yes," Esther agreed. "Overwhelming, but also scary."

Rebecca had been filled with trepidation last week, so she understood Esther's response. This time Rebecca had other concerns. She'd struggled to keep her eyes off Abner the whole trip. He sat one seat in front of her and across the aisle, so she had a perfect view. And he couldn't see her staring unless he turned around, which he often did to check on one of his brothers or flash Rebecca a smile. Then she flicked her gaze to the nearest window or pretended to be studying something near him.

They managed to gather their luggage and exit the

train together. Each boy had on a backpack and carried a sleeping bag.

"Can I carry those bags for you?" Abner said to Rebecca and Esther.

Rebecca shook her head. "If we're each holding one boy's hand, Esther and I should carry our own suitcases so you have a free hand for James."

"*Danke* for offering," Esther said shyly.

Abner smiled at her. "You're quite welcome."

Rebecca studied the two of them. Did Abner seem attracted to Esther? Was his smile extra wide, or had she only imagined it? *Stop it, Rebecca. You broke up with him, so you have no right to care who he smiles at.* But emotions overpowered her mental scolding. Even worse, Esther was strikingly beautiful, making it even harder for Rebecca to tame her jealousy.

She pushed the thoughts aside to concentrate on Philip, who was yanking her hand and trying to catch up with his older brothers. She let herself be dragged close to James, who was shouting and pointing at an incoming train.

Rebecca smiled at his excitement, and when she glanced up, Abner had a fond smile as he watched her. When their eyes met, his twinkled.

"Last week I thought your idea of bringing the boys was brilliant. Now I'm not so sure." He smiled to show he was teasing. "As long as we get them all to the apartment, I can relax."

"I hope so." But she wasn't so sure. Four boys cooped up inside a small apartment? That might be a disaster. And she doubted the adults would get any time to relax. What had she been thinking? She'd wanted to help Adah, but she hadn't considered the boys' liveliness.

When they entered the soaring waiting room, the boys' mouths hung open.

"How big are those?" Peter pointed to the arched windows. He'd always loved math, especially weights and measurements.

Rebecca wished she hadn't packed the guidebook in the suitcase. She could use it to answer some of their questions.

Abner stared at the windows as if mentally measuring them. "They're definitely taller than Miller's silo. Perhaps around fifty-five or sixty feet high."

"Wow!" Peter stood transfixed. Then he lifted his fingers and squinted while he measured sections.

Rebecca hadn't expected the train station to provide a math lesson, but she was pleased that Peter had come up with the idea. "How many pillars are there from here to that entrance door?" she asked James.

"Can I count the people?" Philip asked.

Abner laughed. "If you can do that, go right ahead." He and Rebecca exchanged a glance, and her heart pitter-pattered at his special smile.

Esther, her mouth hanging open, had stopped to stare at the ceiling, much the same way Rebecca had last week.

Rebecca hurried over. "You might want to keep moving so you don't get knocked over," she suggested.

John pulled at Esther's hand to catch up with his brothers, and she hurried along, her head swiveling from side to side to take in everything she passed. As they reached the others, Abner's cell phone rang.

He pulled it out of his pocket. "It's Paul." He held it up to his ear for a few moments. "That door's straight ahead. We'll be right out." He clicked the phone off and stuck it in his pocket. "We need to hurry. The limo's going to be pulling out front shortly."

Abner guided Esther to the correct outside door and onto the busy sidewalk. Rebecca trailed behind with his *mamm* and the two youngest boys. Abner might only be acting polite, but Rebecca struggled with seeing him being so solicitous to someone else. And deep inside, she wanted to switch places with Esther. Why were her desires always the opposite of her resolution to stay away from him?

When the limo pulled to the curb, Abner ushered Esther in first. His brothers pushed past him, and loud exclamations came from inside, as they ricocheted around, rocking the limo. Abner helped his *mamm* climb in before turning to Rebecca. She stepped aside to evade his touch, and hurt flared in his eyes.

"This'll be fun for her, don't you think?" Abner glanced past her to Esther, who was gawking at the minibar, the tinted windows, the plush seats.

"Yes, it was quite an experience the first time." Even now, it was nice to travel in this luxury, but she wasn't as overawed with everything the way she'd been last week or like Esther was now. Had she already grown jaded?

Abner tried not to look at Rebecca, because each time he did the pain of her rejection tore through him. He busied himself getting his brothers calmed down and settled into their seats. He opened the refrigerator to *ooh*s and *aah*s.

"If you stay in your seats, you may each have something to drink," he said. Paul must have ordered the refrigerator stocked for children because in addition to water, he'd added an assortment of small juice boxes. After he handed bottled water to the adults, he picked up four juice boxes.

"I want that one," Philip howled when Abner handed the raspberry one to James.

Mamm intervened. "You'll take whatever one you get and be grateful."

Philip thrust out his lower lip when Abner offered him grape, but he took it. Then he watched his brothers unwrap their straws and poke them into the cardboard containers. He tried to do the same, but his movements were clumsy.

Abner reached out and grabbed the juice box. The last thing they needed was a fountain of juice squirting up all over the limousine. After he inserted the straw, he started to hand it back to Philip, who was sitting with his arms crossed and a mutinous expression on his face.

"I can do it myself." Philip disliked having help because he was the youngest. He always wanted to prove himself as equal to his older brothers. He hoped that wouldn't become an issue here in the city.

"I know you can." Abner tried to soothe his little brother's hurt feelings. "Now you have to hold this gently because otherwise all the juice will squirt out."

His brother's eyes lit up. Not a good sign. Abner kept a light, firm hold on the container, but Philip reached out and snatched it. Juice squirted out all over Abner's hand and his brother's shirt.

Esther, who was sitting closest to the minibar, grabbed several napkins. She wrapped one around Abner's hand to stop the flow of juice before it reached the carpet. Then she began scrubbing at Philip's shirt.

"Danke." Abner gave her a grateful smile. If it hadn't been for her quick thinking, they'd have had a purple puddle on the limo floor. He wiped his hand and the juice box.

"Ach, this will stain unless we soak it soon," she said.

"We're almost at the apartment," Abner told her, although with New York traffic, moving a few blocks could take forever.

Once Esther had done her best to sop up the juice on Philip's clothes, she reached for the cloth napkin Abner was holding. "I'll wash these and return them when they're clean."

Abner smiled. "I appreciate that and your quick action. You saved us from having a major disaster."

Esther's cheeks flushed, and she ducked her head. *"Ach,* it was nothing."

Nearby Rebecca shifted in her seat, drawing his attention. Her gaze flicked from him to Esther and back again. He wasn't positive, but was that a flash of jealousy in her eyes?

Maybe she cared for him more than she'd been showing lately. But she had nothing to be jealous about. Yes, Esther was pretty and sweet, but he had no interest in her. He'd given away his heart to one woman, and he had eyes only for her.

Chapter Twelve

When they arrived at the apartment, Rebecca sorted out the chaos of baggage and who would sleep where, while Abner helped his *mamm* to bed and Esther scrubbed Philip's shirt and the napkins in the kitchen sink.

When Abner emerged from the bedroom, Rebecca pointed to three sleeping bags and backpacks by the door. "Peter, James, and John will stay with you. They've agreed to take turns on the couch. Philip wanted to stay with your *mamm*, so he can sleep out here in the living room with me or on the floor beside your *mamm*'s bed."

"You're sleeping in the living room?"

"Someone has to. Esther needs a bed. I changed all the sheets before we left, so it's all ready for her."

His smile expressed his gratitude. "I hadn't thought about where everyone would sleep, so I appreciate you working it all out." He glanced toward the kitchen where Esther was still scrubbing away at the fabric. "It's very kind of you to give up your bed for Esther, but will you be comfortable enough on the couch?"

"Of course." Rebecca's feelings had gone up and down like a roller coaster ever since Abner had first smiled at Esther. Now he was staring not at Esther, but at her, with much more than gratitude in his eyes, making her almost dizzy. She lowered her eyes and tried to keep her rioting emotions in check. "Did you want to take the boys' bags to your apartment?"

"Good idea." Was it her imagination, or did he sound downcast at her suggestion?

Across the room, all four boys knelt on the couch, watching cars and people down below.

"Look," Philip said. "An ambulance!"

"There's a police car." James pointed to the left.

"And look at all those trucks." John bounced on the couch. "They look like toys."

"I see a cat in that window." Peter motioned toward the building directly opposite. "It's strange you can look right into people's windows. I wonder if they're looking back at us."

"They probably are," Abner said dryly before turning to Rebecca. "Well, it doesn't look like I'll be getting any help carrying the luggage. They're too engrossed in sightseeing. At least they're doing it indoors. I'd hate to think of letting them loose on the city streets."

"I agree." Trying to watch all of them and keep them together had been wearing.

Abner slung his duffel over his shoulder and then hooked two of the backpacks over his other arm. As he reached for the third one, Rebecca picked it up. "I can help you carry some of this."

He looked about to protest, but then he shrugged. "*Danke* for your help."

His smile made her stomach flip. Maybe this wasn't such a good idea. She bent to reach for a sleeping bag, and their hands collided. Rebecca jerked away. This definitely wasn't a good idea.

With hurt in his voice, Abner said, "I'll take these two." He indicated the two sleeping bags closest to him.

Rebecca nodded and picked up the other one. She accompanied him down the hall and offered to hold the sleeping bags while he unlocked his apartment door. He held them up by the ties, giving her plenty of space to grasp them without touching him.

While she dumped the boys' gear onto the couch, Abner let the two backpacks slide down his arms. With her hands empty and his back facing her, Rebecca longed to touch his broad shoulders, the biceps that flexed as he dropped the backpacks. She grasped the sides of her black half apron, pleating and twisting the fabric to prevent herself from reaching out. Her conscience rang alarm bells. They shouldn't be alone in the apartment together. "I—I should go," she said before she turned and rushed out the door.

Abner spun around, but before he could say a word, Rebecca had disappeared. The door slammed shut behind her. She couldn't get away from him fast enough. He trudged to the bedroom to set down his duffel bag. One foolish mistake in the past had destroyed everything.

He took his time unpacking his few items to calm himself and make it easier to face Rebecca. He'd purposely not looked at her when he set the items on the couch, but he'd been acutely aware of her presence, her every move. She'd been right to flee. But it still hurt.

He debated about staying in the apartment, but he should make sure *Mamm* and the boys were all right. Or at least that was one reason for returning. The other was to spend more time around Rebecca. Abner exited and locked up the apartment. As he headed down the hall, he almost ran into Paul, who was carrying two huge bags.

Abner hurried toward him. "Let me help you with those."

"It's all right. I've got them."

"If you're sure." Abner rushed over to open the apartment door.

Paul crossed the room and set the bags on the table. "I figured the kids might like hamburgers and fries for their first meal here." He lifted out some small red boxes. "I got them special meal boxes with toys in them."

"They'll like that." Abner called his brothers, and Esther came out of the kitchen to help organize them around the table.

"Whoa!" Paul stopped dead, one hand in the bag. "Who's this?"

Abner gestured toward Paul. "Esther, this is my boss, Paul Campbell." He debated about waving a hand in front of Paul's face to snap him out of his daze. "And Paul, this is Esther Allgyer. She's Sarah's cousin."

"Well, hellooo." Paul eyed Esther appreciatively, and her cheeks colored. "Why haven't I met you before?"

Esther dipped her head shyly. "I only arrived this morning."

Paul let go of the container he'd picked up, and it dropped back in the bag. Then he extended his hand. When Esther shook it, he engulfed her hand with his other one and held on long after they were done shaking. Esther didn't seem eager to pull away. Abner got a sick feeling in his stomach. He hoped he hadn't made a mistake in introducing them.

Turning on his charisma, Paul gave her a dazzling smile. "So, lovely Esther, what brings you to New York City?"

"I came to help with the boys."

"Of course. They must be a handful. Are you interested in acting, by any chance? You'd be a perfect fit for our movie."

"Movie?" Tiny furrows appeared above Esther's nose, and she removed her hand from his.

Abner's nausea grew. Paul had used a similar line on him, without the extra dose of dazzling teeth and theatrical charm.

"Paul makes movies," Abner explained, but he hoped his tone conveyed a warning.

Rebecca, who had been headed toward the table, stopped and pinched her lips together. She lowered her eyes, and her cheeks turned cherry red.

No doubt she was remembering almost starring in one. No, not almost. She *had* starred in one. One they'd both been assured would be destroyed.

Although Rebecca's fingers plucked nervously at the sides of her apron, her voice was steady when she told Paul, "Esther lives in upstate New York, but when she came to visit Sarah's family in Pennsylvania, Adah asked her to stay to watch the boys."

Esther flashed Rebecca a grateful glance. She evidently appreciated her not mentioning the real reason for the visit and Esther's recent heartbreak.

Paul brightened. "If you're new to the city, I'd be happy to show you around—if you'd like?"

Abner stood to one side, his jaw clenched. No way would he let Esther go anywhere with Paul alone.

Rebecca must have had the same thought. "Esther is responsible for the boys. That will take up a significant amount of time. Besides, she's already been baptized and is with the church." Her icy tone conveyed the message that Esther was off-limits.

Paul's bewildered expression showed he didn't understand the last part of the message, so Abner explained, "Rebecca means Esther is finished with *Rumschpringa.*"

"So she can't do any more running around?" Paul managed to tear his gaze away from Esther to glance at Abner for confirmation.

"That's right." He was pretty sure she wouldn't go out with an *Englischer* in any case.

Esther, who had been silent until now, put her hands on her hips. "I'm capable of speaking for myself, and I believe Paul directed his question to me."

He turned to her with a brilliant smile. "Yes, I did. So, what do you say, doll?"

The spark of attraction in Esther's eye worried Abner, but to his surprise, she said, "I appreciate your kindness, but I came to the city to care for the boys. I'm afraid I must do my duty."

"So bring the kids along. I know this terrific toy

store. They'd love it." His grin begged her to say *yes*. "And all women like to shop, right?"

Sounding every bit like a stern schoolmarm, Rebecca interrupted. "The boys aren't on vacation. They have to complete their lessons."

Esther shot Rebecca a quelling glance. "I'm not sure the children will have time for toy stores. They need to focus on their education. As for me, I'm not much of a shopper. I make or grow most of what I need, so I rarely shop, except for occasional visits to the grocery store or secondhand store."

"I like self-sufficient women. I don't think I've ever met a woman who didn't like to shop. You're amazing."

Esther beamed but lowered her head. "Perhaps we should eat before the food gets cold." She busied herself helping Philip, who was struggling to open his box.

Paul, his eyes still fixed on her, set the rest of the food on the table. Because the table only had four chairs, the adults had to take their meals and sit in the living room. With the open floor plan, they could keep an eye on the boys. Esther took a meal in for Adah, and she was gone so long Abner wondered if she planned to stay in there until Paul left.

Well, if Paul was interested in Esther, he'd have some competition for her attention—four small boys and her faith. Her reaction to Paul, though, worried Abner. Of course, Esther wouldn't consider an *Englischer*. From the little he remembered of her when she'd lived in the area before her family moved to New York state, she'd been both shy and conservative. She didn't seem to have changed in the short time he'd seen her since she arrived, and Abner had a duty to protect her.

At least Paul hadn't made a play for Rebecca. Perhaps because he assumed they were dating. Maybe if he discovered they'd broken up, he might express interest. The very thought made Abner's blood boil. Paul had better not get any ideas about pursuing Rebecca. He'd be sure to draw that line. Paul needed to understand both girls were off-limits.

Rebecca had planned to take a meal to Adah, but seeing the desperation in Esther's eyes, she sent her a silent signal by motioning to Adah's room with her chin. Esther's relieved nod told her she'd made the right choice.

After Esther hurried off, Rebecca took her own food and headed for a living room chair. She wished she could avoid eating here too. Being around Paul reminded her of times best forgotten, and she'd just fled from Abner. Her face hot, she reluctantly chose the chair beside Abner. Her only other choice was sitting beside Paul on the couch.

As soon as she sank into the sling chair, she regretted it. Paul had taken a spot on the couch that gave him the best view of the hallway leading to the bedroom. He focused his attention there, even though he was talking to Abner. When Esther returned, she'd be forced to sit next to him, although sitting across from him might be equally as uncomfortable.

As soon as Rebecca settled into the sling chair, Abner bowed his head, and the boys copied him. Paul surprised her by closing his eyes while they all prayed silently, but as soon as the prayer ended, he went back to watching the hallway.

Beside her, Abner swiveled his head to follow Paul's

line of sight, and his jaw tightened. Was Abner jealous of Paul's attention to Esther? Rebecca ached inside at the thought Abner might be interested in Esther.

Philip unwrapped the toy airplane from his meal box and zoomed it around John's hamburger.

"Stop it!" John swatted at the plane but hit Philip's hand instead.

Philip wailed. "He hit me! He hit me!"

Before Rebecca could get out of the chair, Esther raced from the bedroom. She hugged Philip. "What's going on here?"

"I didn't mean to hit him," John said, close to tears. "I just wanted to get his airplane out of the way so I could eat."

"Perhaps you could tell Philip that."

"I'm sorry, Philip. I didn't mean to hurt you. Will you forgive me?"

Philip sniffled and nodded.

"It also sounded like you might have disturbed your brother," Esther told Philip.

After scrubbing at his eyes with his fist, Philip said, "I'm sorry, John."

"It's all right. I know you were excited about the plane."

Then Esther reached for the airplane. "I'll put this in a safe place until after we're all finished eating. That way everyone can have a peaceful meal." She set the airplane on one of the high built-in shelves on the living room wall.

In a low voice, Paul said, "She's amazing, isn't she? The way she handled that argument was brilliant."

Rebecca wanted to snap that she settled bigger disagreements than that every day at school, but doing so would be *hochmut*, so she remained silent. She didn't care too much that Paul appeared besotted with Esther, but it bothered her that Abner seemed to agree with Paul. He'd swiveled his head to watch, and he'd been smiling the whole time at Esther's handling of his brothers.

"I think it would be best if I ate right here," she said. "That way I can be sure everyone behaves." Although her tone held a bit of sternness, the smile she bestowed on each boy in turn was guaranteed to take the sting out of the reprimand.

Peter jumped to his feet. "You can sit here, Esther. I'm almost done, and I don't mind standing."

"That's very thoughtful of you," Esther said.

The boys appeared overjoyed at having her sit with them, although Paul looked disappointed.

After he finished his lunch, Paul glanced at his watch and then rose. Although he barely took his eyes off Esther, he directed his comments to Abner. "Look, I know you came a day early to get everyone settled in, but Herman wants you at the studio this afternoon."

Abner scrunched up his face. "Seriously?"

Paul nodded. "Lunch was supposed to be a bribe."

"It didn't work." Abner crumpled his hamburger paper in his fist and shoved the last few french fries into his mouth before he stood with a sigh.

Paul watched Esther lean over to wipe ketchup from Philip's chin. "She's really good at that, isn't she?" he said quietly.

Abner followed Paul's gaze. "Yes, she is. That's why *Mamm* hired her to watch the boys."

"I could watch her all day," he said dreamily. "But

I'd better get you over to the studio before Herman explodes."

"Yes, I definitely think we should go." The steeliness in Abner's tone indicated his words held a deeper meaning.

Rebecca hoped his warning only meant he wanted to protect Esther from the movie business, but what if it was also a warning to stay away from Esther because Abner was interested in her?

Chapter Thirteen

Abner wanted to drag Paul by the arm to get him out of the apartment. He also hoped this wouldn't mean Paul would show up all week. If he did, Abner would need to find a way to protect Esther.

Paul's cell phone beeped. "We're on our way," he said and clicked the phone shut. "I told you he was impatient." He checked his watch. "The limo was supposed to be here by now." He tapped his foot and sighed. "If we don't hurry, he'll take his irritation out on one of the actors."

A few minutes later, the limo glided to the curb. Abner climbed inside, wishing he could spend the afternoon at the apartment with Rebecca instead.

By the time they arrived at the studio, Herman was shouting at an actress. "Can't you get anything right? You're supposed to be naive. Forget that you've lived here all your life. Imagine growing up on a farm."

"I did," she said, her voice wobbly. "You don't know anything about farm life. I grew up on a farm. We're not the backward hicks you're imagining."

"The Amish are," Herman insisted, his face red.

"That's not true," Paul said, striding over to join the argument.

Abner hung back, not wanting to get drawn into a disagreement about his community, but the actress spotted him and pointed. "Ask him if you don't believe me."

If only he could disappear or be invisible. Abner held up a hand. "I'm not sure I'd be a good judge of what should be in movies."

"I don't mean movies. I mean real life." The girl had her hands and teeth clenched, but tears of anger spurted from her eyes.

When she lifted her balled fists to scrub at the tears, Herman screeched, "Stop!" He grabbed for her hands, imprisoning them in his huge ones. "You'll ruin your makeup." He turned to Paul. "Grab something to mop up her face, and get the makeup man in here pronto."

Paul reached for a small rag and dabbed under the girl's eyes, where black pools of liquid made her resemble a raccoon. Abner stared fascinated as black stripes trickled down her face.

The girl turned on him. "What are you staring at?"

Abner averted his eyes. "Sorry," he mumbled. He wondered if he should point out that she had her dress on backward. Perhaps the *Englisch* viewers wouldn't know or care, but if Herman planned to pay such a huge sum of money for Abner's advice, he should probably let them know.

After Paul returned with the makeup artist, Abner pulled him aside and explained.

To his relief, Paul laughed. "It figures. I'll have her change it as soon as her makeup's fixed. Maybe Herman will be glad we delayed the shoot, otherwise he would have had to redo all the scenes with the backward dress in them." He clapped Abner on the back. "Thanks for the tip."

"Speaking of tips," Abner said, "I'm not sure why the other girl is wearing a white apron while she's working in the kitchen. Those white aprons are only for church. If she's in the kitchen, she should have on a work apron."

Paul pulled a small notebook from his pocket. "Describe what she should be wearing."

"A black work apron that covers her whole dress. It ties in the back. Like the apron Esther was wearing when she came out of my *mamm*'s bedroom. I'm sure you noticed the change."

"I did." The dreamy look came back into Paul's eyes. "She had on a black apron that tied at the waist when I arrived."

"Actually, those don't tie at the waist. They're pinned in the back."

"Pinned? I hope they use safety pins."

Abner shook his head. "No, straight pins."

Paul winced. "Poor Esther. Don't they get poked when they sit down?"

"I don't know. I've never worn an apron, but I've never heard anyone complain or say *ouch*, so I guess not."

Paul stared off into the distance. "I remember what the black apron looks like. She only turned around once to put something on a shelf, but I'm pretty sure it tied at the waist."

"That's right. The work apron is tied rather than pinned."

"And it had this keyhole opening above the tie."

For someone who'd only had a brief glimpse of Esther's back, he had a precise memory of minor details. Abner definitely needed to keep an eye on Paul when he was around Esther. Better yet, he should do his best to prevent them from spending any time together. No matter how committed Esther was to her faith, Paul was skilled at talking people into things.

After Paul left to confer with Herman, Zander wandered over. "Missed you on the set on Friday. We could have used your help to settle a few disputes."

"Me?"

"Yeah, you. I grew up in the city, but even I can tell some of Herman's ideas are farfetched. He and Everly fought about everything."

"Everly?"

"Yeah, the blonde over there." Zander jabbed his thumb in the direction of the girl who'd been crying when Abner walked in. "She keeps claiming she grew up on a farm. Not sure I believe her, although I do know she came from some hick town in the Midwest."

"I hope they get it resolved." *Without my help.* The last thing Abner wanted to do was to get tangled up in arguments between Herman and the cast.

"Me too. All this back-and-forth stuff has been messing up the shooting schedule. Looks like they may have to extend it another week if we can't get this scene shot on time."

Abner hoped it wouldn't mean they'd expect him to stay longer too. The sooner he found a way to get rid of that film of Rebecca and him, the sooner he could go home for good.

* * *

After Abner left, Esther cleaned up after the meal while Rebecca gathered the boys to begin lessons. Philip begged to be included, so she tried to give him some easy tasks to keep him occupied. Having only four students instead of thirty made it much easier to move through the lessons rapidly, although they were sometimes distracted by sirens or other loud noises outside the window. They were packing away their school books when Paul showed up with large buckets of fried chicken for supper.

Turning her back to Paul, Rebecca encouraged Esther to retreat to the bedroom. *I'll bring supper back to you and Adah*, she mouthed.

"Thank you," Esther whispered. In a louder voice, she announced, "I'll keep Adah company tonight for the meal. She shouldn't be alone."

The tension lines on Abner's face relaxed, and behind Paul's back, he smiled at Esther and mouthed his thanks.

Paul didn't stay long once he discovered Esther wouldn't be joining them. "I'll get you tomorrow morning," he told Abner. Then he turned to Rebecca. "What time do you need the limo to pick you up?"

"They want Adah at the clinic at nine."

"I'll arrive here a little after eight then, so you can use the limo. Abner and I can take a taxi."

As soon as the door closed behind Paul, Abner leaned back against it and expelled a loud breath. "That was fast thinking to send Esther in to eat supper with *Mamm*."

"It worked well earlier today, so I hoped it would again. I realized after I said it, though, that this evening your *mamm*'s supposed to only eat and drink what's on her special sheet because her treatment begins tomorrow."

Abner pressed his lips together and rubbed his forehead. Rebecca longed to reach out and comfort him but settled for a silent prayer.

"I hope this will help," Abner said. "I read and reread the papers they gave her, and the first clinical trials had some promising results, but the list of possible side effects and complications has me worried."

"We have to leave it in God's hands," Rebecca reminded him. That would be hard for Abner to do because he was still angry at God over his *dat*'s death. If only she could find a way to help him see the truth.

Abner's brothers had gathered around the buckets of chicken.

Sniffing the air, James said, "That for sure and certain smells delicious."

"I'm so hungry," Philip whined, clutching his stomach.

Rebecca smiled. "Sounds like someone's hinting that we should be eating."

"That's more than a hint." Abner studied his brothers. "Manners, please." Then he turned to Rebecca. "Would you mind feeding them while I check on *Mamm* and Esther?"

Actually, I would mind. Not feeding the boys. That's no problem. I do mind your going after Esther.

She hesitated so long, he said, "It's all right. I can take care of their meal. Or I can ask Esther to do it."

"No, I'm fine with it. I can even call Esther."

"I don't mind." Abner strode past her and down the

hall. He knocked on his *mamm*'s door. Then he pushed open the door. "Paul's gone, so it's safe to come out."

He used the teasing tone Rebecca loved. Would he and Esther have as much fun joking around as Rebecca and Abner used to have?

"*Mamm*, what should we get you for dinner? And do you want to come out and join us at the table?"

"I'd like that." Adah's voice sounded thin and weak. "I believe I'm supposed to have broth or clear liquids after eight tonight, but I might as well start now." She emerged from the bedroom, leaning on Esther's arm.

"Are you all right?" Rebecca asked. Adah looked pale and wan.

"Traveling really drains me." Adah made her way to the table and sank onto a chair. "I must admit I'm quite nervous about tomorrow, so that's taking a toll on me too."

Rebecca wished she could ease Adah's burden. "Could we pray with you?"

Adah gave her a grateful glance. "I'd appreciate that. Where two or three are gathered in My name…"

"…there am I in the midst of them," Rebecca finished.

She went over and took Adah's hand, and Esther reached for her other hand. The boys clasped hands to form a circle, leaving room for Abner. James and Peter held out their hands to include their older brother, but he hesitated.

Please, Lord, Rebecca prayed, *help Abner to join our circle and our prayer.*

With his younger brothers holding out their hands and looking at him expectantly, Abner couldn't hurt them or *Mamm*—or Rebecca—by refusing. Reluctantly, he crossed the room and completed the connection. They all bowed their heads.

Rebecca's gentle voice rose to heaven, and Abner hoped God was listening.

"Dear Father, we come before You to ask for Your mercy for Adah. Please calm her nerves and prepare her body and spirit for the procedure tomorrow. We pray that this treatment will heal her, but we will accept Your will whatever the outcome. In Jesus's name, Amen."

No, I won't accept whatever outcome occurs. I want Mamm to get well. No other option is acceptable. Despite his lack of acceptance, Abner appreciated the warmth and strength that flowed around the circle through their hands. The unity of purpose. And Rebecca's prayer had touched his heart. If only he had her simple faith. Her trust in God radiated from each word she spoke.

Mamm's eyes brimmed with tears as she squeezed Rebecca's hand, and Abner's heart contracted. His *mamm* often said she considered Rebecca to be the daughter she never had. Abner had hoped...

He turned away to hide his own damp eyes. If he lost *Mamm* and Rebecca...

Chapter Fourteen

The next morning Rebecca woke with a crick in her neck. She'd fallen asleep praying for Adah's health. Each time she woke during the night, she repeated her prayers.

Predawn grayness blanketed the sky, but lights shone through the window when Rebecca lifted the blinds. Neon lights flashed, car lights made white or red blurs in the street below, and lights flickered in windows and over doorways. So unlike the dawn at home as she padded out to the henhouse to gather eggs.

After she dressed for the day and had her morning devotions, she went into the kitchen to tackle the cookstove. Now that she'd mastered its secrets, she should be able to prepare a decent breakfast.

Philip bounded out of the bedroom and joined her in the kitchen.

"Do you want to help?" she asked.

His face broke into a grin. "Everybody always says I'm too little."

"I don't think you are," Rebecca assured him. She

brought a chair into the kitchen so he could crack eggs and stir in the milk. His enthusiasm meant eggs splashed out of the bowl or dribbled down the sides, but that was a small price to pay for teaching him a new skill. And who knew whether he might have to help around the house. If his *mamm* didn't make it…

As if he'd picked up on her thoughts, Philip glanced up at her, his lower lip wobbling. "*Mamm* said she's going to stay in the hospital tonight. I'll miss her." His eyes searched Rebecca's. "Will she be all right?"

Trying to project a confidence she didn't quite feel, Rebecca started to nod, but stopped. She shouldn't give him an answer when she had no idea of the outcome. Only God knew that.

She'd been heating the skillet, but she waited to pour in the eggs. Instead she wrapped an arm around Philip's shoulders. "Should we pray for her?"

Blinking back tears, he nodded. He bowed his head and spoke softly, reverently. "Dear Jesus, please take care of *Mamm* and make her better. Amen."

Rebecca followed with a simple prayer for his *mamm*'s healing. When she was done, Philip threw his arms around Rebecca and hugged her.

"Jesus will take care of her, right?"

Her throat tight, Rebecca nodded.

The butter sizzling in the pan had burned. The heat must be too high or she'd left it on too long. Rebecca sighed and lifted the skillet off the burner. She wiped out the burned butter and waited for the pan to cool a bit before she added more. This stove kept issuing her challenges, but Rebecca was determined to win.

By the time Esther and Adah entered the kitchen,

Rebecca had managed to make a skillet of scrambled eggs, and she'd browned toast in the toaster. She turned to Philip. "Could you go and call your brothers?"

After he took off down the hall, Rebecca turned to Adah. "What can I get you?"

Adah, even more ashen than she'd been last night, shook her head. "I'll just have a cup of hot water."

The apartment door banged open, and all four boys raced in, followed by Abner. Rebecca wished she could ease the tension lines etched into his face. He barely looked at her or Esther. Instead he focused all his attention on his mother.

"Good morning, *Mamm*. How are you feeling?"

"A bit weak and tired, but I'm sure I'll be fine." Her wan smile did little to remove the concerned frown wrinkling his brow.

Rebecca served breakfast, hoping it would distract him from his worries. He gave her a brief smile when she handed him a plate.

"Looks like you figured out the stove."

She laughed. "We'll see. Eggs aren't that hard to cook."

He managed a grin. "You're having better luck than you did with the oatmeal."

"True." She tapped a finger on the center of the stovetop. "I think I've conquered this part of the beast. The oven is next."

"Can't wait to see you subdue that."

It wouldn't be tonight, though. Rebecca kept silent about that because she didn't want to remind Abner his *mamm* would be spending the night at the hospital.

Luckily, Paul knocked on the door and handed out

donuts to the boys, which distracted everyone from their concerns. Adah held up a hand to let him know she was passing on the donuts. Paul nodded, but barely seemed to see her.

Instead, he concentrated on Esther. "You're looking lovely this morning," he said as he held out the box of donuts so she could select one. Then he turned to Rebecca. "You do too, of course." Then he offered the box to Abner. "You ready?"

Abner nodded, selected a donut, and after giving his *mamm* a special look, he headed out the door, triggering Rebecca to pray for him as well as Adah.

Rebecca stood by the table to eat, and as soon as she finished, she brushed the crumbs from the table into her hand. Then she started to pick up her plate, but Esther stopped her.

"Just leave it. I'll take care of all that. I know you two need to leave."

Adah pushed herself to her feet, and Rebecca took her arm. They headed down to the limo and were whisked off to the clinic.

"I don't know what time I'll be done," Rebecca told the driver. She didn't want to think about riding home alone. Right now, her only focus was helping Adah through her first day of treatment. As the limo drove off, Rebecca escorted Adah into the clinic, sending up prayers for Abner's peace of mind and Adah's healing.

Throughout the morning, Abner struggled to keep his mind on his work. If Rebecca had a cell phone, he could contact her, find out how *Mamm* was doing.

"Yo, Abner," Herman barked, "you planning to stare off into space the rest of the day?"

Abner faced him. "Did you have something you wanted me to do?"

"Yeah." Ordinarily, the sarcasm in Herman's tone would have squashed Abner's daydreaming, but he was too absorbed in hoping—possibly even praying—that *Mamm*'s treatment was destroying the cancer.

Paul stepped closer and waved a hand in front of Abner's face. "Look, man, I know you're worried about your mom and all, but we need to keep moving."

"Work with the new actors for the next episode. Their accents are atrocious," Herman yelled. "Paul, give him that script and put him in one of the available rooms."

Paul grabbed a script and ushered Abner and several actors down the hall. He opened the door to a room with a large wooden table surrounded by chairs, and everyone trooped in.

Motioning to one end of the table, he said to Abner, "Sit here at the head of the table, so everyone can see you." He set down a blue booklet held together with two brads. "Here's your copy of the script."

Abner stared at the booklet blankly. "What am I supposed to do with this?"

Paul opened it up. "I'm guessing you've never seen a script before?" When Abner shook his head, he pointed to several names in capital letters. "This tells who's speaking. The dialogue is underneath each of their names. See how these are typed in narrower columns? The longer information is setting and stage directions."

The page in front of Abner indicated "EXT. WOODS BEHIND REBECCA'S HOUSE—MIDNIGHT." His heart contracted at the name Rebecca. Were they building this story around her?

"See," Paul said, "EXT. means an exterior scene. In this case, it'll be in the woods behind Rebecca's house. Make sense?"

Paul's explanation made sense, but he was still concerned about Rebecca. "Could they use a different name?"

"Not at this point," Paul said. "Parts of the first episode have already been shot. Her name's been mentioned multiple times." He clapped Abner on the shoulder. "Don't worry. We didn't use your name. We wanted something swoon-worthy."

When Abner had been considering signing the contract, Herman had said they'd want to change his name.

"Usually in romances, the hero has a short, strong name, but Herman wanted *Jonathan* because it can be drawn out during the romantic scenes." Paul mimicked a breathless falsetto voice. "Ooh, Jon-a-than…" He fluttered his eyelashes for dramatic effect.

Abner clamped his teeth on his lower lip to control his anger. Although he told himself the Rebecca Paul was imitating wasn't his Rebecca—no, not his Rebecca anymore—it still pained him to think they'd used her name for this mockery of Amish values. He stayed silent while Paul ran his finger down the page. If he let his temper take control, he might never get to destroy the film.

Paul stopped at a longer line of text. "For example, this tells the actors what to do."

Rebecca removes her head covering and lets her

hair down. Jonathan runs his fingers through her hair before kissing her.

Biting down on his lip wasn't enough to keep Abner silent. "That would never happen," he burst out. "No Amish woman would take off her *kapp* like that. Never, ever."

Paul patted his shoulder. "This is TV, not real life."

Abner shoved back his chair. "You said you wanted me here to make this show authentic. I don't agree with what you're doing or with having actors pretending to be Amish. I'd never have agreed to this if I hadn't been blackmailed."

Several people gasped.

"That's a strong word. Herman was only trying to persuade you to cooperate."

"No, it was blackmail. And I'm only here for one reason. To get that screen test destroyed."

"Which it will be. If you cooperate." The velvety tone of Paul's voice didn't match the underlying steel of his words. He left no doubt of the threat beneath his soothing speech.

"I've been cooperating, but if you want this to be authentic, then this"—Abner stabbed a finger at the description—"needs to be taken out. It's not realistic."

"I'll talk to Herman, but I'm pretty sure he's going to want to have those lovely long tresses cascading about the actress's shoulders. But you've given me an idea. It might play well to have Jonathan act shocked at first." Paul closed his eyes and rubbed a finger over his chin. "The innocence. The shock. The temptation. The fumbling awkwardness." He opened his eyes. "I like it, and I bet Herman will too."

"No." Abner had to make his point. "You don't understand. Her *kapp* isn't just a hat or head covering. It's a *prayer* covering. It's sacred." He took a deep breath to calm his distress at treating this so casually, so... Words failed him. "The *kapp* symbolizes submission to God, being in a prayerful attitude of humility to the Lord at all times."

Paul held up a hand. "Okay, okay, I'll discuss it with the screenwriters. Just calm down. We have a lot of work to do." He massaged his forehead. "I suggest you not read the stage directions or anything other than dialogue for now."

Abner would try to follow directions, but it wouldn't be easy.

"Basically, what we need you to do is read the dialogue, so each actor can hear how it sounds. Then have them repeat it, and you correct their mistakes. Like you've been doing with the rest of the cast during rehearsals. Herman thought it might be more efficient to do it beforehand, so they can concentrate on other things during rehearsals."

They got most of the way through the script before the lunchbreak. As soon as everyone else left the room, Abner called the hospital. The woman who answered put him on hold. When she clicked back on, she said, "Your mother is doing as well as expected. She'll be staying overnight."

"I know. Thank you for the update."

"Visiting hours are until eight tonight," she said before clicking off the phone.

Abner stood there, phone pressed to his ear, listening to the silence. She hadn't said *Mamm* was "doing well."

What did "doing as well as expected" mean? Had there been some problems or complications?

Zander came up behind him and slapped him on the back. "How come you're hiding out here?" He took one look at Abner's face and asked, "Something wrong?"

How did Abner answer that? Lots of things were wrong. This job at the studio. His relationship with Rebecca. His guilt over his role in the screen test. The clip Herman was holding hostage. *Mamm* having cancer. Abner's relationship to God. Where did he even start?

Zander tilted his head and raised a bushy eyebrow to convey he was curious and awaiting an answer. His eyes held acceptance.

Abner shook his cell phone. "I just called the hospital to see how *Ma*—my mother was doing. She has cancer."

"Aww…that's rough, man. Sorry." Zander patted Abner on the shoulder, his movements a bit awkward. "What'd they say?"

"That's what I'm trying to figure out. I have no idea what 'doing as well as expected' means."

"Sounds like legalese for 'She's fine.' Most doctors don't like to state facts straight out in case they're wrong. You know, so you don't sue them later."

"We wouldn't do that. The Amish don't believe in suing people."

"You don't?" This time both of Zander's thick eyebrows crawled toward his forehead. "You mean you wouldn't take them to court if the treatment hurt or killed her?"

"Of course not. Besides, *Mamm* agreed to the treatment, so she's the only person responsible for her decision."

"But the doctors and—" Zander rubbed his forehead. "Wait a minute. Why am I trying to talk you into suing a clinic? Especially when it sounds as if your mother's fine." He wrapped a friendly arm around Abner's shoulders. "Come on. Let's go get some lunch."

After they filled their plates, Abner headed for two chairs in a secluded corner. He hoped to talk privately with Zander.

"This private enough for you, man? Seems like we're on a desert island."

Abner shrugged and took a seat with his back facing the room. Zander sank into the chair opposite him. They both tore into their sandwiches and chewed silently for a while.

Then Zander swallowed and eyed Abner closely. "I take it you want to talk about something and don't want anyone to overhear? Or are you just upset about your mom and not up for company?"

"*Jah*, I mean, yeah." Actually, both of those were true, but he wanted some information he hoped Zander could give him. He tried to make his question casual. "Can you tell me more about this cloud thing?" At Zander's confused look, he added, "You said all the films in production would be on a cloud."

Zander's lips quirked. "You mean *in the cloud*?"

"I guess so."

"You know how people store stuff on their computers? Well, maybe with you being Amish and all, you wouldn't know about that."

Abner didn't correct him. Although he didn't own a computer, he had friends who did. They might know all about this cloud stuff, but he didn't want to wait until the weekend.

"It's a little confusing," Zander said. "I don't really understand it all myself, but it's a type of remote storage you can use for bigger files. Storing films and TV shows can take up a huge amount of space, so another company hosts all the files for you. They split them up among different servers. It's a little confusing, but all we need to know is that we have enough room to store things."

The main word that stuck out to Abner was *remote*. "You mean they're stored far away from here?" If so, he never should have come to New York.

"Yep." Zander took a sip of his soda.

"Then how do you work on them?"

"You ever used a computer?"

Abner nodded.

"You know how you can get information from all over the world right there on your screen?" After Abner indicated he did, Zander went on. "It's the same with the cloud. You don't have to go anywhere. You can access it all from your computer."

"If you wanted to get rid of a movie or something, you could erase it from the cloud?"

"It's called *delete*, but yeah, it could be done pretty easily."

"So, if you wanted to delete something on the cloud, what would you do?"

Zander looked up as a hand descended on Abner's shoulder. "Hey, Paul."

Abner's whole body went rigid as Paul gripped his shoulder. Had he heard what they were discussing?

Chapter Fifteen

When Paul interrupted Abner's discussion with Zander, Abner froze in place, his mind racing. How long had Paul been there? How much of the conversation had he overheard?

If he had heard, he gave no indication of it. His hand remained steady on Abner's shoulder. "As soon as you're done with lunch, Herman wants you to watch a run-through of a scene he's not happy with."

Unable to croak out a word, Abner nodded. After Paul left, Abner set the rest of his sandwich down on his plate. He'd lost his appetite. If he tried to eat a bite, he'd get sick.

"You okay?" Zander asked. When Abner didn't answer, he said, "Listen, it sounds like you need help to find and delete a video. Am I right?"

Abner glanced over his shoulder to be sure nobody else was within hearing distance.

"Chill, man. No one's around."

"Yes," Abner said hurriedly. "I do."

"Wow, you sound kinda desperate. You're not in some dirty movie or something, are you?"

"Of course not," Abner snapped, then regretted it. "Sorry, Zander. No, it's nothing like that."

"Gotcha. Didn't mean to offend you, but with how secretive you were being and all, well, it kinda seemed"— he shrugged—"I don't know, like it might be something you were ashamed of."

Abner was ashamed of it, but not for the reasons Zander suspected. "It's just that—"

Herman barged through the door. "Abner, what's taking you so long? Do you have any idea how much every minute's delay costs? Maybe I should start to dock your pay for every minute wasted." He laughed sarcastically. "You'd already have lost every penny."

Abner jumped to his feet.

"Catch you later, man," Zander said. "I'll try to help if I possibly can."

"Thanks," Abner called over his shoulder as he hurried out the door after Herman.

The cast was already in place on the stage when Abner walked in. A barn interior formed the backdrop on one side of the stage. The other side had a courting buggy with a background of fields behind it.

"We're doing one final run-through of the teaser before we shoot." Herman lasered in on Abner. "This still doesn't feel right to me. It has to be perfect. We're running this in all our ads."

Paul beckoned to Abner. "Come stand over here by us. We want to hear all your comments."

"Yes," Herman added. "Stop them to correct any accents or actions that don't look authentic. With so many

competing fake Amish shows, I want *Bonnet Rippers*
to stand out as genuine."

Bonnet Rippers? Abner cringed. What did that
mean? Did it have anything to do with the scene he'd
criticized earlier? And how could the show be genuine
if everyone in it was only pretending to be Amish? All
these contradictions confused him.

As Herman gave the cast some final instructions,
Abner's mind wandered to *Mamm*. He wished he could
leave now to see how she was doing. Zander seemed to
think she was fine, but he'd rather see for himself. Then
the scene unfolding before him drove all thoughts of
Mamm from his head.

Jonathan convinced Rebecca to join other couples—
both Amish and *Englisch*—who were slow dancing on
the straw-strewn floor, and the two of them stumbled
around, tripping over each other's feet until Jonathan
whispered to Rebecca that they should cool off outside.
They moved to the buggy, where Jonathan wrapped his
arms around Rebecca and bent his head for an amo-
rous kiss.

Abner closed his eyes to squeeze out the vision, the
memories. Had Herman done this purposely to torture
him?

The whole scene was the exact same one he and
Rebecca had shared. The scene Herman's cameraman
had taped.

At a loud slap, Abner's eyes popped open. Rebecca
hadn't slapped him. She'd pulled away from him with
a shocked expression on her pretty face, and then she'd
demanded he take her home immediately.

Onstage, a hysterical Rebecca, her chest heaving

with sobs, shouted at Jonathan never to touch her again. Turning away from him, she insisted he take her home. "I'll never speak to you again," she spat out through clenched teeth.

Abner's Rebecca had not screamed or railed at him. Instead, she'd gone deadly silent and stared at him with sorrow-filled eyes.

Now Abner was the one with sorrow-filled eyes. He'd done everything the actor Jonathan had acted out. The couple onstage had dramatized his and Rebecca's story for the world to see, revealing Abner's sinfulness and selfishness. How could he have been such a fool? In his faulty imagination, those acts had been justifiable, but now viewing them from afar, his actions had been inexcusable. Heat rose from Abner's chest and splashed across his face. He ran one finger under his collar and pressed the other to his burning cheeks.

Oh, dear God, please forgive me. No wonder Rebecca broke up with me. Nauseous, he turned away from the stage unable to watch the last moments of the story. He had to get out of here. He'd excused his behavior to himself, whitewashed the version in his mind. But seeing it played out on the stage sickened him. He had to apologize to Rebecca, but this time his repentance would be genuine.

"You all right, man?" Paul asked. "You look ill."

Abner was tempted to brush it off and hide his true feelings, but he forced himself to be honest. "Seeing that scene…" How could he explain how horrible, how guilty it made him feel?

"Not easy watching your past?"

No, it wasn't. It was horrible. And watching this also

added to his fears about the clip Herman had of Rebecca and him. These actors seemed too slick and polished. He and Rebecca had been more awkward and genuine. What if Herman decided the original film was better and more authentic? And he substituted that instead?

Rebecca spent the morning in the waiting room. Someone had taken Adah back soon after they'd arrived to begin the procedure. Although Rebecca had brought a book along with her, she couldn't concentrate. Her mind kept wandering to Adah, wondering how the treatment was going, and to Abner, worrying about him getting caught up in worldly things. Finally, she bowed her head and turned all her worries over to the Lord.

Afterward she became engrossed in her book and didn't look up until the doctor entered the room.

Rebecca jumped up, and her book tumbled to the floor. "How is she? How did everything go?"

"We're still monitoring Mrs. Lapp, but she appears to be doing well."

"May I see her now?"

The doctor shook her head. "She won't be able to have visitors for several hours. We'd suggest going home now. You can visit later, perhaps this evening, if she's up to it."

"Would it be all right to bring her children then?"

"Not tonight. We've found most patients are too exhausted for visitors."

Rebecca had spent time with several people in the community following radiation and chemo, so she understood some people weren't ready for company. The doctor had explained that, unlike chemo, which killed both good and bad cells, this procedure was more targeted, so Rebecca had hoped it wouldn't be as draining.

The children would want to see their *mamm*, though. "How soon do you think it'll be before the children can come?"

"With this being an experimental treatment, we can't really say. Recovery times have varied. Possibly later in the week, but we'll have to wait and see how she reacts to the procedure before making that decision."

"I see." Rebecca bent and scooped up the book. "Should we call first before we come?"

"That would be wise." The doctor bid her good day and headed off.

Rebecca stood where she was for a moment to thank God the first treatment had gone well. Then after praying for Adah's health, she slipped on her coat and headed out to hail a taxi. Paul had told her to call the limo, but she had no phone and didn't want to feel obligated to Herman and Paul.

She tried to remember what she'd seen Paul do. She stood near the curb but jumped back when car tires splashed slush in her direction. The frigid wind bit through her coat, and her toes iced inside her shoes. She held up her arm, but cabs zipped past. Finally, one pulled close, double parking beside the cars along the sidewalk.

Rebecca waded through the gray slush, which sloshed over her shoes and slid inside. She should have worn boots.

"Where to?" the taxi driver asked as she climbed into the backseat.

Rebecca gave him the address and leaned back

against the seat, grateful for the heat blasting from the front of the car. She wished she had a way to contact Abner to let him know the procedure was over and seemed to have gone well. She'd have to wait until he came home.

"You an actress?" the driver asked, startling her from her thoughts. "You been in any films? Or are you working on a TV show?"

"What? *Ach*, no. Definitely not." Although maybe that wasn't true, she had been in a film that one time.

"So how come you're in that get-up?"

"Excuse me? Get-up?"

"You know, those clothes?"

"I'm Amish," she explained. "We dress like this as part of our religious beliefs, to honor God."

"Oh, yeah. I remember now. I seen some people like you on one of those Amish TV shows. My ex liked to watch it. It ran at the same time as one of my favorite shows, so she didn't see much of it." He cackled. "Maybe that's why she's my ex."

Rebecca had no idea what to say to that, but he didn't seem bothered by her lack of response.

"So you doing that running-away thing?"

"I'm not running from anything." Then it dawned on her. "You mean *Rumschpringa*?"

"Yeah, that's it. Seems like a lot of you Amish run away so's you can drink and party."

"I'm not—" The warning bell in her conscience clanged. As recently as last month she'd been one of them, although she'd given it all up. "Not anymore. I'm done with all that."

"You mean yer going to dress like that for the rest of your life?"

"Yes, I plan to."

"A little hard to get a man when you dress like that, ain't it?"

"No, I'm looking for a man who respects me."

The cab driver pulled over in front of the apartment building. "Well, good luck finding someone who loves and *respects* you." He said the word *respects* as if it was a dirty word.

"Thank you," Rebecca said as she paid him. Then she headed inside. She couldn't wait to take off her damp shoes, but her mind was still on the taxi driver's words. She thought she'd found someone who did both. But Abner's trickery proved he hadn't respected her. She was still deep in thought as she entered the hotel lobby.

"Good afternoon, Ms. Zook," the doorman greeted her, startling her from her reverie.

Rebecca had no idea how he knew who she was. "I'm sorry, but I don't know your name."

"Gerald Johnson, ma'am."

She smiled at him. "It's nice to meet you. Good afternoon, Mr. Johnson."

When she entered the elevator, the man automatically pushed the correct button for her floor. It almost seemed like magic.

When Rebecca walked into the apartment, Esther looked a bit frazzled. "How is Adah?" she asked.

The boys gathered around her to hear about their *mamm*.

Rebecca repeated the information she'd been told at the clinic. "How were the boys?"

"They kept me busy." Esther's tired smile indicated there was more behind her words, but Rebecca would wait until the boys weren't around to ask.

She squatted down to address the boys. "Since I'm back earlier than expected, let's start your lessons now. I want you all to gather your books and meet me in the living room in five minutes."

After the boys scattered, she kept her voice low. "What happened?"

Esther just waved her hand vaguely. "Four boys in one small room for most of the day. It's not easy finding things to keep them occupied. And they really missed their *mamm* and kept asking questions about her I couldn't answer."

"That must have been so hard on them—and you."

"Yes, they missed her last week, but chores and school filled their days, so they had less time to worry. Here, we can't go outside, so they didn't know what to do with themselves. Oh, and we lost Philip for half an hour."

"You did?" Rebecca tried not to sound too startled. How could that even be possible in such a small apartment? He'd either be hiding under the bed or in the closet.

"We searched frantically for him. I even opened the door to Abner's apartment to check in there, but he was nowhere to be found. I didn't have any way to contact you or Abner, so I decided to ask the front desk for help."

"*Ach*, I didn't realize you'd had such a frightening time. How did you find him?"

"I gathered the other boys, and we headed to the

door. I planned to go downstairs to the desk to report him missing. I was frantic but praying God would keep him safe." Esther paused to draw in a calming breath. "I don't think I've ever been so worried in my life."

"I can imagine." Rebecca would have been scared too. Being in a strange city, knowing nobody, and having no idea where to look. At home, they'd have friends and family nearby to help and to spot any missing children wandering past. Here they were alone. In a city full of strangers.

"Anyway, when we got to the elevator, the door opened. Philip was inside grinning. According to the elevator operator, he'd been having the time of his life, pushing buttons, riding up and down, and talking to the other occupants."

Rebecca hid a grin. Philip was an adventure seeker like Abner and his *dat*. He kept things lively at home and loved to tease. "I'm so glad you found him."

"I am too," Esther said. "I gave him a lecture on the dangers of running off, but I don't think he paid much attention."

No, most likely he hadn't, knowing Philip.

Rebecca wished she could offer some advice on handling Philip, but she wasn't sure what would work.

"I was thinking," Esther said hesitantly, "with you being so good with children and needing to teach them lessons every day, what if I went to the clinic to be with Adah and you stayed here?"

Rebecca would miss the chance to be with Adah, although with her treatments maybe she wouldn't actually see much of her. And Esther definitely deserved a break after her scare this morning. "I'd be happy to watch the boys. It would give me more time for lessons. I guess we can't ask Adah about switching places, but let's check with Abner when he gets home."

"Danke." Esther sounded so relieved, Rebecca was glad she'd agreed.

When Paul and Abner headed to the hospital at the end of the day, Paul said, "Look, I didn't mean to upset you today. I know you probably think I was insensitive about the *kapp*, but I really didn't understand it was sacred. I probably should have, so I'm sorry."

Abner nodded. He still wasn't sure Paul really understood, but at least he was trying. Now that Paul had opened the conversation about this topic, Abner took the opportunity to express some of his conflicting feelings. "Herman keeps saying he wants the show to be genuine, but it can't be. Not with actors faking that they're Amish. They don't believe what we believe, so they're only going through the motions."

Paul pinned him with a look. "What do you believe?"

Under Paul's searching gaze, Abner squirmed. Did he want to know what all Amish believed? Or was he specifically putting Abner on the spot?

When Abner didn't answer, Paul said, "The reason I'm asking is because you seem to have one foot in each world. You dress the part and defend Amish beliefs, yet you don't seem too committed to your faith. You also don't have that peace and serenity that your mother, Rebecca, and Esther have." Paul studied Abner's face. "Do you even believe in God?"

Abner crossed his arms in front of his chest as if to ward off a blow. "Of course," he said automatically, but

Paul had hit him where it hurt. He'd exposed the core of Abner's pain. And unbelief.

"You sure?"

Paul's question forced Abner to confront the tangled mass of feelings he'd buried since his *dat* died. "It's not that I don't believe in God," he said finally, "it's that I don't trust Him."

"So you believe He exists, but you don't believe He cares about you?"

Abner wanted to hunch over to protect himself from that blow, but he made himself sit up and take Paul's comments as a man. An honest man. One who wasn't hiding from the truth.

If anyone had asked Abner, *Do you believe God cares about you?* he would have snapped back a quick *yes*. But sitting here facing Paul's insightful question, Abner couldn't avoid the truth. Not only was he angry with God, he also didn't believe he was worthy of God's love.

Abner lowered his head. No way could he meet Paul's eyes. But Paul had asked an important question, and he deserved an answer. "I've used my anger at God as an excuse to be rebellious. I've done so much over these past few years that makes me feel ashamed." And seeing the actors portray him and Rebecca had only piled on even more guilt. It was hard to believe God could forgive his mistakes, sins, and rebellion.

"I guess the reason I'm asking," Paul said, "is because I'm struggling with the same thing. When I was a boy attending church with my grandmother, I prayed and turned my life over to God. But over the years, I drifted away. If God's keeping a record, mine's much darker than yours, and my shame's much greater."

Abner had no idea what Paul had done, but he was well aware of his own shortcomings. "I'm not sure God compares our sins."

"I guess the important thing is that His mercy can cover all our sins," Paul said. "I've been reading the Bible Sarah's *mamm* gave me, and I've started back to church. Seems to me the worst sin must be rebelling against God and refusing to accept His forgiveness, because that's what separates us from God."

Paul lowered his head into his hands, so his words came out muffled. "I've been doing that all of my adult life. I keep feeling this nudge to confess it all to God and start a new life, all clean and forgiven. Then I get sidetracked because I think of all the things I'd need to give up. As much as I hate to admit it, the pull of God in my life is overpowered by the lure of the world."

Abner understood completely. He had the same struggles. When Rebecca talked to him about joining the church, Abner was eager to put his old life and his sins behind him and surrender his will to God's. But when he was away from Rebecca, his intentions were waylaid by temptations.

As the limo pulled in front of the hospital, Paul's words echoed in Abner's ears. *The worst sin is rebelling against God and refusing to accept His forgiveness.* And that's exactly what he'd been doing ever since *Dat* died. Could he ever come to the place where his human desires didn't hold him back from committing himself to God, the church, and the community? Now that he didn't have Rebecca urging him, the decision would be his, and his alone.

Chapter Sixteen

The following morning, Rebecca woke eager to start lessons with the boys. A few minutes later, she hoped the older three boys would be less rambunctious than their younger brother. Esther's lecture had not made much of an impression on Philip, who was bouncing around the living room, jumping off furniture, and causing a ruckus. Esther went in to start breakfast, leaving Rebecca to deal with the chaos.

Abner knocked on the door and herded his three younger brothers into the apartment. Last night he'd seemed so depressed and distant, and this morning he never met her eyes. He must be upset about his *mamm*. The clinic hadn't let him see her last night.

"Are you all right?" she asked him. "I know it's hard not being able to see your *mamm*."

"It is," he agreed, staring at the carpet. Suddenly, he looked up and gazed at her with such sorrow that she wanted to reach out and comfort him. "I need to talk to you. Not now, with *Mamm* so ill, but sometime soon."

"All right."

His *mamm*, then, wasn't the only source of his sadness. It almost seemed as if he were also carrying a load of guilt. Rebecca took a guess. Perhaps working at the studio was weighing on his conscience. Before she could ask, Paul arrived, carrying a paper bag. The boys came rushing over and almost knocked him over, hoping for donuts.

"Settle down," Abner scolded. "If you maul Paul, he might not come back."

"Maul Paul," Philip sing-songed. "That rhymes."

"A little good-natured greeting like this would never scare me away." Paul tousled each boy's hair with his free hand, then opened the bag.

Philip peeked inside and groaned. "I wanted donuts."

"I'll keep that in mind for the next time."

Rebecca leaned down. "Be polite," she reminded him in a quiet voice.

"I'm sorry," he said. "Thank you for bringing those—" He gestured to the bag.

"Croissants," Paul supplied. "I thought maybe the adults might like a treat today."

"Are they sweet?" Philip asked.

"Not really." Paul smiled. "They're more like bread. A very buttery, rich bread."

"In that case, I'll skip making toast this morning," Esther said.

Paul turned startled eyes toward the kitchen. "I'm so sorry. I didn't realize you were there. You're—"

He sounded as if he'd been about to compliment her, but then changed his mind. Perhaps Abner had set some boundaries or talked to him about *hochmut*.

Either way, it was a welcome change. His attention

remained on her, and Esther's awkward movements made it clear she was uncomfortable.

Rebecca intervened. "Why don't you set the bag on the table, Paul?" She pulled out a chair whose back faced the kitchen. "And have a seat."

With no excuse to keep staring at Esther, Paul did what Rebecca asked. Abner's eyes twinkled briefly at her success, and they shared a secret half-smile before his eyes grew shuttered and despondent.

The boys crowded around the table, but Rebecca said, "Because the adults need to leave soon and we don't, I think it would be nice if you waited for the second seating."

Philip crossed his arms. "But we're hungry too."

Abner spoke up. "Rebecca's right. It'll be good for you to learn patience."

"I don't want to learn patience." Philip huffed and flopped down on the couch.

"But God would want you to."

Rebecca's eyes widened. She could picture Esther or Adah saying that. But Abner? Perhaps with his *mamm* away, he felt the need to take her place.

When Esther brought the food to the table, Paul hopped up to take the dishes from her. Then he pulled out her chair and helped seat her. Esther appeared bemused. Following the prayer, she only picked at her food and peeked at Paul out of the corner of her eye whenever he looked in another direction.

Philip strolled over to the table and stared at the food with puppy-dog eyes. If he had been a puppy, Rebecca would have had a hard time resisting. She steeled herself against his pleading and wished she hadn't suggested the boys wait. Because Abner had backed her up, though, she didn't feel she could go back on her directive.

When no one offered him anything, Philip's face fell. He looked about ready to slink off. Then he brightened. "Guess what, Paul? I rode the elevator for a long time yesterday."

That served as Esther's cue to tell the whole story, and Paul hung on every word. Esther turned to Philip when she was done. "I hope you'll be *gut* and not give Rebecca any scares." Then she turned back to Paul. "At home, I always have family and friends I can call on. Yesterday I panicked when I realized I didn't know a soul. I had no idea what to do or who to call."

His eyes sympathetic, Paul reached into his pocket and pulled out a gold monogrammed case. He flipped it open and took out two cards. He handed one to Esther and the other to Rebecca. "That has my cell phone number as well the studio telephone number. If either of you are ever in distress, please call."

Rebecca didn't point out it was a bit difficult to call when neither of them had phones, but she held her tongue and slid the card into her dress pocket.

Then he turned his attention back to Esther. "I'm so sorry you went through that yesterday. I'm glad you'll be safe at the clinic today. We'll drop you off and pick you up, so I—we won't have to worry." At Esther's soft *danke*, Paul's eyes grew tender.

Rebecca cleared her throat. "I'm sure you're all as eager to be off as these young men are to eat."

"*Ach,*" Esther said, "and me not ready yet. I still need to change my apron."

"You look fine the way you are," Paul assured her.

Esther shook her head. "I can't go out in my work apron."

"Oh, that's right," Paul said. "You need a half apron like Rebecca's wearing."

Esther's eyebrows rose. "How did you know that?"

"I pay attention to details." Paul gave her a special smile, and Esther looked impressed when she turned to go. Then he turned to Rebecca. "I am curious about why you have on a half apron today."

Rebecca busied herself with getting the boys situated at the table and hoped he'd let the matter drop, but once Abner's brothers were in their places and devouring their breakfasts, Paul was still staring at her with a question in his eyes.

"The boys are used to seeing me dressed like this when I teach." Rebecca wanted to end there, but her conscience wouldn't allow her to tell a half-truth. "And it's always good to be prepared for an outing if the weather improves." She kept her words quiet so the boys didn't overhear.

"The sun is supposed to come out later." Paul followed her cue of speaking softly. "Maybe you'll all enjoy a bit of sightseeing."

Rebecca nodded. "I don't want to raise their hopes and then dash them if the weather goes bad."

"I understand." Although he was talking to her, Paul's gaze remained fixed on the hallway where Esther had disappeared. His face lit up when she reappeared. "Time to go," he said to Abner, who'd been sitting on the couch, his expression one of deep regret.

Rebecca wished they'd had more time to talk. She

disliked seeing Abner so down. But maybe God was working in his heart and showing him the dangers of working at the studio. If that happened, though, what would that mean for his *mamm*?

When they arrived at the clinic, Abner got out with Esther. "I just want to check on *Mamm* because I didn't get to see her last night."

"Not sure we can sit here idling for long," Paul said. "If we're not here when you come out, we'll be circling the block. Just wait right here for us."

"Thanks," Abner said. "I appreciate it."

"No problem, man. Hope she's doing well." Although Abner assumed Paul meant *Mamm*, the way his eyes followed Esther, Abner couldn't quite be sure.

Esther was already at the desk inquiring about *Mamm* by the time Abner caught up with her. "We can visit with her, but only for a short while."

Abner followed her to the elevator. When they reached the room, Esther stepped back. "I know you don't have much time, so I'll let you go in alone."

"Danke." He appreciated her thoughtfulness. He opened the door and entered.

Mamm lay on the bed closest to the door, her eyes closed, and so still she appeared— The blankets over her rose and fell. Oh, thank the Lord, she was breathing.

The fear constricting his chest eased, and he slid into the chair beside the bed. He reached for her hand and tucked it in both of his. He rubbed her icy hand between his palms, trying to warm it. Even though he'd stuffed his hands in his pockets when he was outside, they'd gotten chilly, but they were still warmer than *Mamm*'s.

Seeing her here in a hospital bed instead of their homey kitchen was hard. He squeezed his eyes shut. When he opened them, *Mamm* was watching him.

"Praying?" she asked in a whispery voice that seemed drained of energy.

He should have been. He sent up a quick, silent prayer for healing before he nodded. "How are you feeling?"

"Ex-haus-ted." She dragged each syllable out.

"I'm so sorry."

"Don't be," she said. "They said I'm in a fight for my life. I feel like I'm losing." Each word came out slow and breathless.

"Don't say that," Abner said. "You're here to win."

Mamm's barely perceptible nod broke his heart. "You can do it," Abner assured her.

"I hope so." She tilted her head slightly so she could look up into his eyes. "How are the boys?"

"They're missing you." Abner told her about Philip and the croissants.

"Rebecca does such a wonderful job with him. I'm glad she agreed…" Her voice trailed off.

"Agreed to what?" Abner asked.

"Never mind." Her wan smile indicated she wanted to change the subject.

Abner obliged by telling her about Philip's escapades in the elevator. He managed to get a slight chuckle from her. "I hope he doesn't give Esther too much trouble."

"Actually, Rebecca and Esther switched places. Rebecca is taking care of the boys, and Esther is waiting outside to keep you company."

"I'll miss Rebecca. I enjoy her company, but I feel better knowing she's teaching them their lessons."

Abner stood. "I need to get to work now, but I'm sure Esther will take good care of you." He kissed *Mamm* on the forehead, and her eyes closed before he straightened.

In the hallway, he told Esther he'd explained about her taking Rebecca's place. "And I told her about Philip's elevator ride yesterday. That made her laugh."

"It's funnier now than it was yesterday," Esther admitted. "I'll take good care of her, and I'll find a phone and call you if anything changes."

"I'd appreciate that." Abner smiled at her and then turned and headed for the elevator. He wished he could stay and encourage *Mamm* in her fight. He dreaded going to work. What if *Mamm* lost the battle while he was gone?

"You okay?" Paul asked as Abner got into the limo.

Abner shook his head. "She's so weak she could barely keep her eyes open. What if this treatment doesn't work? After all, it's still in the early stages of clinical trials. What if they find out it has dangerous side effects they didn't know about?"

Paul held up a hand. "Hey, slow down a minute. You're talking so fast I'm having trouble keeping up. Take it one question at a time."

"There is only one question—one big question. Will *Mamm* recover?"

"That's a huge question," Paul said. "And only time will reveal the answer."

"I know." Abner rubbed his forehead. "I just wish I had some assurance this experimental treatment will help."

"Look at it this way. What assurance do you have

that you'll be around after this moment? There are no guarantees."

"True." That didn't ease his worries about *Mamm*, though.

"You probably don't read the newspapers," Paul continued, "but people die every day of heart attacks, freak accidents, and mass murders. The only thing you can do is—"

"Pray. That's what *Mamm* relies on for every crisis." *But I have no right to ask for favors from a God I've rejected.*

"Why don't we try that?" Paul suggested.

"You want to try praying?" Abner stared at Paul, dumbfounded.

Paul rubbed the back of his neck. "Well, actually, yeah, I do. The thing is…last night after we talked, I went home and got down on my knees to ask God for forgiveness. It's been a long time since I prayed, so I wasn't sure I got it right. I guess it's good that God hears what's in your heart even if your words are uncertain."

Was Paul saying he'd turned his life over to God? Abner stared at him.

"Anyway, when I woke up this morning, I felt different. Cleansed. Renewed. Changed. Now that I've asked God to take charge of my life, though, I have to decide about my future. I'm not sure I can continue to work on projects with Herman."

Abner couldn't believe it. "You really prayed about this?"

Paul nodded. "You know, I keep thinking of Saul in the Bible and how he persecuted the Christians. Then he gets blinded by a light, and God talks to him. He's never the same after that. His name is changed to Paul, and he becomes one of the greatest Christians." Paul laughed. "Not that I'm saying I'm going to become a great Christian example or anything, but last night I did feel like I experienced that flash of light."

Paul wasn't the only one who'd been hit by lightning. Abner felt as if his whole world had been upended. *If Paul experienced such a dramatic transformation from one night on his knees, what does this mean for me?* Abner weighed the possibilities in his mind. Was it time for him to make a similar commitment? He shook his head. Somehow whenever he thought about getting right with God, doubts and roadblocks always arose.

"My job's the thorniest issue," Paul said. "Does God want me to give it up completely? If He does, what would I do instead? I have no other talents or experience."

Abner couldn't speak for God, but he did have a question of his own. "I can't speak for God, of course, but why would He want you to give up a profession you're good at? That makes no sense to me."

"Hmm…" Paul pulled on his lower lip. "Maybe you're right. I have a huge reach through the TV audience. Maybe I could use that to influence people. This Amish project might be perfect. We'd have to give it a different spin, make it reflect your real beliefs."

That's exactly what Abner had been trying to convey when they discussed the sacredness of the *kapp*. It would be great if the show wasn't totally fake. Paul's changes could have a ripple effect. But how ironic would it be if Paul, with his new faith, contributed more spiritual elements to the show than Abner did?

Chapter Seventeen

After the boys went to bed, Abner asked Esther to watch them, but he left the connecting door open between the apartments. Philip had curled up on the sofa and fallen asleep.

Abner's heart tripped faster each time Rebecca smiled at his brother, because then she turned to him with sparkling eyes. She'd let him hold her hand several times today. Maybe she was softening.

The brilliance of her smile lit up the room and his heart. Until he remembered he needed to make his own confession.

Abner swallowed hard as the actors' portrayals of Rebecca and him flitted through his mind in full color. "I apologized a few weeks ago, but I didn't realize how deeply hurtful my behavior had been to you. I ignored your protests and insisted on pushing you into going against your conscience for my own self-interest. I claimed to love you, but everything I did was selfish."

Her questioning glance made him wonder if she'd misunderstood his apology, but he plunged on. He had to try one more time to make things right between them. "Ever since I realized what the situation looked like from your viewpoint, I've been sick inside, and I knew I had to apologize. Will you forgive me?"

"I already did."

"No, I mean forgive not only my actions, but also my self-centeredness."

"Abner, I'm not sure why you're questioning my forgiveness, but I don't hold anything against you." She tilted her head to one side. "Unless you mean can we begin our relationship again? If that's what you're aiming for, the answer is *no*."

Abner hung his head. She'd misunderstood his point. He hadn't told her this to rekindle their love. Seeing those actors reenacting the scene made him sure and certain he wasn't worthy of her love. Or God's.

The next day at lunchbreak, Zander strolled up to Abner. "Wanna go for a walk?" Zander laughed at Abner's surprise and motioned to the door with his head. "I have something I want to show you."

As soon as they were alone, Zander said, "I managed to bypass the password on Herman's computer the other night after everyone left. If his office is unlocked, we can delete that file for you."

"You can?" Abner couldn't believe it. Maybe at long last, he'd have a clear conscience. At least about the film clip.

They headed down the hall, and after checking that the coast was clear, they ducked into the office. Zander locked the door and sat down at the computer.

He scrolled through a list. "Any idea the name of this thing you're looking for?"

Abner shrugged. "No. I'm sorry."

"Let's type your name in the search bar and see if we get any hits." Zander tapped several keys. "Bingo. I think this might be it." He clicked on an icon.

Abner's face filled the screen. The camera pulled back to reveal the barn behind him. It followed him as he headed toward Rebecca.

"Stop!" he said, unable to bear watching any more.

Zander clicked something, freezing the image of Abner with one hand extended to Rebecca.

"That your girl?" Zander asked. "She's pretty."

"Not anymore," Abner said. "This screen test broke us up." Although yesterday had given him some hope until Rebecca had made it clear they could never be a couple.

"Sorry, man, that bites." A green bar filled in across the top of the screen. "Just checking to be sure this is the only copy."

Abner hadn't even thought about that. "Thank you. I appreciate it."

"Once I've checked, I'll delete this one." Zander glanced over his shoulder. "Would you mind checking to be sure that door is locked? If anyone walks in on us while I'm doing this, I'm dead."

"Dead?"

"Yeah, I'll be in real big trouble. I shouldn't have hacked into Herman's computer."

Abner hadn't thought about that. His only thought had been to see the tape destroyed, but to cause someone else to get in trouble on his behalf? "Forget I asked. I wasn't thinking clearly."

"It's all right, man. Sometimes you have to decide between two bad choices. In cases like this, I always go with the option that seems the least evil or the most helpful."

Zander's logic confused Abner. If something was wrong, you just didn't do it, period. He wished he'd followed that principle when Herman had asked him to act. He didn't want to get someone else in trouble. "I'm not sure about this. If they're both bad, then you shouldn't do either. And I shouldn't have asked you to do something dishonest."

"Don't worry about it. I believe in 'situational ethics.' Like in this case, destroying someone else's property is wrong, but blackmail is much, much worse. And I'm helping out a friend. That means I'll choose to delete this video."

Zander clicked on the video to highlight it. "If anyone finds out I did this, I'll lose my job, but at least I'll have done it for a good cause."

"Wait! Is this illegal?"

"I'm not sure about illegal. Probably is, because I'm destroying someone's IP."

"IP?"

"Intellectual property. I do know it's unethical. But so is blackmail."

"No, don't do this if it's unethical. I'll figure out another way."

"It's no problem," Zander assured him.

But it was. How far had Abner come from the principles he'd been raised to obey? "Never mind. Don't delete it."

"Your call, man, but it'll only take a second."

One second was enough. One second, one thought, one action was often all it took to head down the path of destruction. Or, conversely, to do the right thing.

Each time Rebecca spotted Philip while she was teaching that morning, her heart rejoiced. After yesterday's scare, she sent up prayers of gratitude. Her mind conjured up other possible outcomes, and she thanked God that Philip had been found.

Yesterday had been filled with turmoil. Between fear for Philip and her closeness with Abner, her emotions had roller-coastered from lows to highs. Last night during Abner's apology, Rebecca had clenched her hands in her lap to keep from reaching out to him. After holding hands that afternoon, she'd been tempted to let down her guard, give in to her attraction. But she'd been firm about refusing to restart their relationship, although it had torn her apart inside.

She'd done the right thing. She couldn't consider courting Abner unless he was right with God. If only he'd commit to attending baptismal classes and to joining the church. Not for her sake, but for his own. Once again, she whispered a prayer for Abner's soul.

Then she turned her attention back to the boys who were finishing the work she'd given them. After yesterday's scare, they'd all concentrated hard on their lessons this morning.

"Once you finish that page," she said to Peter, "we'll eat. Then we'll go down to the lobby to call the clinic."

The boys had been begging to see their *mamm*, but so far, the doctor had not given permission. Rebecca hoped they could go today.

The other boys cleaned up their books and supplies while Peter bent his head over his work, with a frown of concentration. Rebecca went to the kitchen to prepare sandwiches but stuck her head out from time to time to be sure the boys were still out there and safe.

After they finished, they crowded into the elevator as it descended to the lobby. When she asked about using a phone, Gerald Johnson pulled out his cell phone and handed it over.

Rebecca called the hospital, and the receptionist informed her in a crisp voice, "The doctor has given the children permission to visit for a short while, but she's been unable to reach Abner Lapp. She needs to speak with him as soon as possible."

"I'll let him know," Rebecca said, and as soon as she hung up, she dialed Abner's number. It went directly to voice mail, so she tried Paul's number.

"I've been trying to reach Abner," she said after Paul picked up the phone. "The doctor said he needs to call as soon as possible. I'm not sure why, because she also gave me permission to bring the boys to see their *mamm*. I don't think she'd do that unless Adah is better."

"I got to lunch a little late today," Paul told her, "but I didn't see Abner anywhere. I'm out running errands now, but I'll pass along your message as soon as I get back to the studio."

"*Danke*. I mean, thank you."

Paul laughed. "I know what *danke* means. I did

spend some time in Amish country." Then he asked, "How are you getting to the hospital?"

"Taxi. I don't think I'm quite ready to navigate buses or the subway." She laughed nervously. Taking a taxi would be expensive, but she'd never ridden a city bus or subway herself. Trying to do it while keeping an eye on four excited boys sounded impossible.

"Herman doesn't need the other limo. I'll send it for you. I'll have the driver park in the garage nearby, so he can be ready whenever you need to leave."

"I appreciate that. We probably won't stay long."

The last time Adah had been so exhausted she could barely keep her eyes open. They'd need to keep this visit brief, according to the doctor's orders.

Rebecca returned the phone to Mr. Johnson and thanked him for his kindness.

A short while later, the limo pulled up, and they headed to the clinic. Rebecca warned the boys about being quiet and not upsetting their *mamm*.

"Maybe we shouldn't tell her about Philip getting lost and riding the elevator," Peter suggested.

"Good idea," Rebecca said. "Let's save that story until she's back home."

But when they arrived at the hospital, a teary-eyed Esther met them in the waiting room and pulled Rebecca aside. "I overheard the medical staff talking about Adah after they left the room. She's had a bad reaction to the treatment, and they're not sure she's going to last the night."

Rebecca felt blindsided. "But the doctor said the children could visit." She bit her lip. She had to be strong for the boys. "I thought," she choked out, "letting the children visit meant Adah was getting better, not worse."

"I guess they wanted the boys to say their good-byes. They haven't been able to reach Abner."

"Paul plans to tell Abner later." But what if he was too late? She had to get him now. "Can you supervise the boys while I go to get him?"

"Of course." Esther called the boys over and squatted down to talk to them.

Rebecca flew out the door and waved to the limo driver, who was still struggling to find a break to pull into traffic. He waited for her to get in.

"Can you take me to the studio as quickly as possible?" she asked.

Once he pulled away from the curb, the driver cut in and out of traffic, ignoring honking horns all around him. In record time, he slid to the curb by the studio, and Rebecca hopped out.

"Can you wait here for me? We'll be headed right back to the clinic."

Rebecca rushed into the studio and asked for Abner. The man at the desk directed her to a room down the hall. She prayed she could find Abner quickly and that they'd make it to the clinic on time.

Abner bent to pick up a script that had fallen onto the floor. He'd take it home with him. Maybe Paul could record his voice speaking the lines so he wouldn't have to come back to the studio. Now that he'd made the decision not to let Zander destroy the film, he needed to fulfill his contract and trust Herman—or at least Paul—

to get rid of the clip. But the more he was here in the studio, the greater his desire to escape.

He'd been foolish to do the screen test in the first place, but he'd be even more foolish to spend time here, when his conscience bothered him every day. He straightened up to find Brooklyn headed in his direction. He'd managed to evade the actress who played Rebecca every time she'd tried to corner him today, but he hadn't been quick enough this time.

"Oooh," Brooklyn purred. "Is it okay if I call you Ab?" She giggled and fluttered her long eyelashes. "You know, as in 'you have great abs'?"

"I don't—" Abner took a step back. He'd been about to say he didn't know what she meant, but her tone and eyes were sending a message that he needed to flee. Now!

"Aww…don't be modest. I bet you do a lot of heavy lifting on the farm, huh?"

She moved closer. He retreated. Soon it became like a dance with her in the lead. One step forward, followed immediately by his step back. Until he ran into the wall. If he didn't do something, her next step would trap him. Herman had warned him not to upset her, but Abner wasn't about to give up his principles to soothe a star's ego.

He gulped. "I have to go." He started to wiggle sideways, but she closed the gap, running a hand along his upper arm.

"Nice." She leaned in, her lips pursed. For the first time in a long time, Abner closed his eyes and sent a prayer heavenward.

Please, God, show me what to do.

He opened his eyes to see Rebecca staring at him. *Rebecca? What was she doing here?*

So much for trying to be polite.

"Rebecca," he shouted and broke free of Brooklyn's grip. He dodged around the actress, but he was too late. The heavy door slammed shut behind Rebecca.

"Hey!" Brooklyn pouted.

"Sorry," he said, "but my girlfriend—" He gestured helplessly to the door. The sound still reverberated in his ears as he yanked it open and chased after Rebecca.

Her stomach roiling, Rebecca raced down the hall, but she couldn't outrun the pictures in her head of Abner with that painted-up girl clinging to him. He'd told her he wasn't being filmed, but was he rehearsing a scene with that—that actress? He had his eyes closed, and the actress was leaning in as if they intended to…to kiss.

He and that girl had been alone together, so if they weren't rehearsing, then she and Abner were— Rebecca shied away from that thought. Either way, she wanted nothing to do with him. For all she knew, he was lying to her again, the way he had the night he'd tricked her into the screen test.

"Rebecca, wait!" Abner pounded after her.

She skidded to a halt. Not because he'd called to her, but because she suddenly recalled she'd come to tell him about Adah. She turned, and he almost ran into her. "You're needed at the hospital. Your *mamm*—" She couldn't finish the sentence.

No matter how angry and sickened she was at him, she couldn't bear to tell him the devastating news. His *dat*'s death had totally destroyed him. How would he deal with his *mamm*'s?

The shock in Abner's eyes revealed he understood what she left unspoken. "She's not doing well?"

That was a major understatement. Rebecca shook her head and hurried out to the limo with Abner on her heels. He climbed in after her, and the driver repeated his harrowing high-speed zigzagging through traffic.

Although Adah should be foremost in her thoughts, the image of Abner with the actress had been burned into Rebecca's mind. She'd broken up with him, so she had no say in his love life, but she felt betrayed.

Abner squirmed on the seat next to her. "Look, Rebecca, what you saw—I know it looked bad."

That was for sure and certain. It not only looked awful, it had cut her deeply. Seeing Abner with someone else drove home the point that she was still totally and completely in love with him.

"Brooklyn is one of the actresses I work with. And Herman caters to her because she's an important actress. He asked me to be careful how I treat her."

She didn't answer, hoping he'd talk about something— anything—else.

"I didn't want anything to do with her, but she kind of trapped me." He looked sheepish. "Like Joseph with Potiphar's wife, you know?"

Abner seemed determined to keep talking about the incident. Perhaps he was trying to distract himself from thinking about his *mamm*.

Rebecca tried to keep the pain from her voice. "What you do is your own business. The important thing is that we get to the clinic quickly."

Chapter Eighteen

Abner had to explain, make her understand what had really happened, but Rebecca's icy glare made it clear she'd misjudged what she'd seen and his behavior disgusted her.

"I don't want you to think I did anything to…that is, Brooklyn tried to—" Abner stumbled to a stop. He couldn't blame this on Brooklyn. He'd been innocent, yes, but saying something bad about someone else to make himself look better bothered him. But if he didn't explain she'd been the aggressor, Rebecca might think he was interested in Brooklyn.

He tried again. "*Englisch* girls are a bit different than Amish girls."

"Evidently." Rebecca's tone was tinged with bitterness.

"And not in a good way. They're more forward for one thing. I wasn't expecting her to, um—" He frowned. "I didn't encourage her."

"You certainly seemed to be enjoying yourself."

"Enjoying myself? I was desperately trying to escape."

Rebecca turned her head away. "Yes," she said sarcastically, "most people keep their eyes closed when they're trying to flee."

"I—I was praying."

She whirled around and pointed a finger at him. "You can fib to me about this—this actress, but I don't ever want you to use God or spiritual things in those lies. I know how you feel about praying, so that excuse won't work. I suggest you get down on your knees and beg God's forgiveness."

"But I was telling the truth," he said as the limo pulled in front of the clinic. Not that she'd ever believe him.

She turned her back on him and stalked to the entrance. Abner hurried after her. Right now, he needed to concentrate on *Mamm*.

As soon as he walked in, a nurse stopped him. "Mr. Lapp, the doctor asked to see you as soon as you arrived."

He followed her down the hallway to the doctor's office. She tapped on the door, and a voice said, "Come in."

"Please have a seat, Mr. Lapp." Her serious tone sent chills down his spine. After a quick recap of his *mamm*'s treatment to date, she said, "We've only ever seen this particular adverse reaction once in the study. A few people responded this way on the first day, but after we injected fluids, they recovered within twenty-four hours."

"What happened to the other patient?"

The doctor gazed off into space. "Our only fatality in the trial so far," she said quietly, her face a mask of pain.

Fatality? The other person with this reaction died?

"What does this mean for *Mamm*?" He had to ask the question, although he dreaded hearing the answer.

"I'm not sure. We've been trying some alternate therapies, but they haven't proven to be effective. Right now, we're treating the symptoms connected with the reaction to make her more comfortable. If she makes it through the night, her chances of survival will be much greater."

He couldn't have heard her right. "*Mamm* might not make it through the night?"

The doctor's sympathetic expression answered his question, but she confirmed it in words. Words that tore into Abner's heart. "I'm so sorry, but that is a definite possibility. I'd suggest you and the family prepare for that."

To the doctor and those conducting this research, *Mamm* was a guinea pig, a test subject—disposable and easily replaced—but to him and his brothers, she was their whole world. The clinic would mourn her as a loss in their statistics, but he and his brothers would lose their family's heart and soul.

When Abner walked out of the doctor's office in a daze, Rebecca regretted turning her back on him earlier. No matter how upset she was over Brooklyn, Abner had to face devastating news. She needed to be there for him as a friend. She'd deal with her own reactions to the almost-kiss later, when she was alone.

"What did they say?" she asked.

He shook his head and mumbled the word *fatality*.

"Abner, look at me," she demanded. Then she waited until he focused his stunned eyes on her before saying, "What did the doctor tell you?"

"*Mamm* might not last the night. Only one other person had a reaction like this, and that patient didn't live."

Rebecca sucked in a breath. Esther had hinted at a serious reaction, but knowing someone else had died— how did you deal with that?

"They're not sure if she'll make it through the night. If she does, her chances for recovery are greater."

With a heavy heart, Rebecca did the only thing she knew how to do in a crisis. Right there in the hallway, she bowed her head.

Dear Lord, please heal Adah. Give the doctors wisdom to deal with this reaction. And keep her safe through the night.

After she opened her eyes, she turned to Abner. "Esther took the boys in to see your *mamm* while I came to get you. They probably shouldn't stay in the room too long." Rebecca headed for the elevator.

"True. They might wear her out." He stopped suddenly. "Do the boys know?"

"I'm not sure what Esther told them." Most likely, seeing their mother's condition, they'd guess.

They took the elevator to Adah's floor, and as they approached, Esther steered four subdued boys from the room. Judging from their faces, the three older boys, with their slumped shoulders and glum expressions, had grasped the truth.

Philip glanced back over his shoulder, a puzzled frown furrowing his forehead. When he caught sight of Abner, he ran toward them. "*Mamm* didn't talk to us. She didn't even open her eyes one time. You always tell me it's rude to ignore people."

Abner pinched his lips together so tightly the blood drained from them. Rebecca wanted to reach out and comfort him. She almost answered for him, but he cleared his throat and swallowed hard.

Squatting down, Abner set his hands on Philip's shoulders. "*Mamm* wasn't being rude. She's very sick." He glanced up at Rebecca as if asking for help to explain the unexplainable.

"Remember when you had the flu a few weeks ago?" His brothers had stayed home from school for two days, and Philip had been sick too. "Your head and stomach and throat hurt, right?"

"*Jah*, but James kept poking me and wouldn't leave me alone."

"You didn't feel like talking then, did you?"

When he shook his head, Rebecca said, "Your *mamm* is even sicker than that, so she can't talk." She debated about telling him more about his *mamm*'s health, but there was always a chance God could work a miracle.

Philip pondered her words for a few minutes. "Then we should be quiet too, because noise hurt my ears and head. Next time, I'll tiptoe."

Rebecca blinked back tears. There might be no next time. She brushed away those doubts and sent up another quick prayer for Adah's healing.

After Philip followed his brothers down the hall, Abner mouthed a *thank you*, but his eyes conveyed more than mere thanks. The adoration in his gaze set

Rebecca's blood on fire. A fire she needed to douse. Especially after what she'd seen today.

Abner hoped his eyes conveyed his appreciation, admiration, and undying love. All the sentiments he couldn't put into words. At least not here. And not now.

Rebecca blushed a beautiful shade of pink, giving him hope that perhaps she wasn't as indifferent to him as she appeared. Right now, though, he needed to concentrate on *Mamm*.

How could he deal with losing her? He steeled himself before he entered the room. *Mamm* lay still and quiet, while machines beeped around her. She'd been hooked up to an IV. Was the steady dripping to keep her alive? She appeared so fragile, and her skin was so pale the dark circles under her closed eyes resembled bruises.

After lowering himself into the chair beside the bed, Abner laid a hand over *Mamm*'s. For the second time that day, Abner prayed. This time his prayer was little more than a groan and a heartfelt cry.

Rebecca sat on the opposite side of the bed, where *Mamm*'s IV hookups attached to her arm, so Rebecca placed a hand on *Mamm*'s shoulder. Rebecca bowed her head, and her lips moved. He appreciated her prayers on *Mamm*'s behalf because no words could adequately express his grief, his fears, his pain.

Several times he tried, but what could he say after he'd rejected God?

They sat in silence for what seemed like hours. Paul came to the door and beckoned to Rebecca. She followed him into the hallway and returned a short time later.

"Paul is going to take Esther and the boys home for dinner," she said softly. "He offered to have dinner sent in to you. And me, if you want me to stay."

Abner shook his head. "You should go with them. No point in staying here when *Mamm* is unresponsive."

"I'm happy to keep you company."

Although he wished she would stay, he had no business asking her to do that. And she should be at the apartment rather than here in a hospital room. "If you don't mind, I'd like some time alone with *Mamm*."

"Of course. I totally understand. But what about a meal?"

"I'm not hungry." In fact, with the way his stomach was roiling, Abner wasn't sure he could even eat a bite.

"If you're sure." Her words came out hesitant and uncertain.

"I am." He had to send her on her way before he ended up begging her to stay.

"I'll be praying," she said softly. "Good-bye, Adah." The way she choked up made him wonder if she was saying her final farewell.

The door closed behind her, leaving Abner alone.

For the next few hours, nurses came and went. The sky outside the window grew dark. Still, Abner sat by the bedside holding *Mamm*'s hand and struggling to pray.

Lord, I know I don't deserve any favors from You, he said at last. *But please, God, don't take her for my brothers' sake. They need someone to care for them, to raise them.*

When he lifted his head, *Mamm*'s eyes were open. He wrapped his hand around hers and gazed at her with misty eyes.

Mamm attempted to squeeze his hand, but her grip was so weak, he barely felt the slight pressure. "We have to trust God. Whatever happens is His will."

No, he wanted to shout. *No, no, no!* Look what God had done when he prayed for *Dat*'s healing. Would the same thing happen?

"Listen to me." *Mamm*'s voice was merely a whisper, and he had to lean close to hear her words. "God has a purpose for everything, son. I know you're struggling with believing that, but turn everything over to God and let Him lead you."

It sounded so simple when *Mamm* said it, but the huge ball of anger inside refused to let go. Abner couldn't turn things over to God.

Mamm's eyes held compassion. "I know it's been hard for you, but lean on God's strength rather than your own."

If this was her last request, he had to comply. He swallowed hard. "I'll try, *Mamm*, I promise."

"Not try, but do." Her voice faded as her eyes closed. Her hand went slack.

Abner bent and kissed her forehead. "I love you, *Mamm*," he choked out, his voice thick with tears.

"Abner?" Rebecca hated to intrude on his private time with his *mamm*, especially if it might be their last time together.

But earlier she'd called the clinic to see if he'd be spending the night. They refused to bend their rules even in a life-and-death situation, so Paul had sent her in the limo. The driver was waiting, and in a few minutes, clinic staff would be coming to enforce the visiting hours.

He didn't move, just stared off into the distance, so she said softly, "Abner, it's time to leave."

She couldn't be sure, but in the dimly lit room, his eyes seem to glimmer with moisture.

"She's not…?" Rebecca couldn't bring herself to say the word.

"I—I'm not sure." His words were thick with unshed tears.

Rebecca joined him at the bedside and pointed to the heart monitor. "See the blips? They're small, but she's still alive."

Abner gripped her hand so tightly it hurt. "Thank God."

"Look." She indicated the slight movement of the bed sheet as Adah's chest rose slightly. "She's breathing." Although it was shallow, the breath indicated his *mamm* was still clinging to life.

Abner sucked some air into his constricted chest and kept his eyes on the sheet. At the next tiny motion, he leaned closer. "The sheet barely fluttered."

The desperation in his words made Rebecca long to comfort him. If only she could remind him of God's love and care. But Abner had turned his back on that source of solace.

A nurse poked her head in the room. "Visiting hours are over. Didn't you hear the announcement?"

"I can't leave," Abner said brokenly. "They said tonight was critical. What if something happens to her during the night? I want to be here."

Compassion in her eyes, the nurse said, "I understand, but she needs her rest. And we may need to do some emergency procedures."

"They let us stay with *Dat* when…" He swallowed hard.

"Many hospitals do allow it, but as an experimental clinic, we need to tightly control many factors. I'm very sorry."

Her heart breaking for Abner, Rebecca tugged lightly at his hand. With great reluctance, he stood. He walked beside her, but he stopped and looked back when they reached the doorway. "I love you, *Mamm*," he whispered. Then shoulders slumped, he headed for the elevator.

"Have you told the studio you won't be there tomorrow?" she asked as they descended. "I'm sure your *mamm* would appreciate your presence here at the clinic."

"If she's even here then," he mumbled.

"I'll be praying she is."

Abner didn't answer, and Rebecca lifted him and his *mamm* up to her Heavenly Father. She prayed that Abner would be able to accept God's will, no matter what the outcome.

Chapter Nineteen

By the time Abner returned to the apartment, his four brothers were sound asleep under Esther's watchful eye. Philip lay on the floor, curled up next to Peter, who had thrown a protective arm around his youngest brother.

"Philip didn't want to sleep in the other apartment alone," she whispered. "I hope letting him stay here was all right."

"Of course." Abner wondered if God had worked it out so all five of them would be in the same place together when they got the worst news of their lives. Maybe Peter had sensed what was about to happen and wrapped his arm around Philip.

After he crawled into bed, Abner tossed and turned for several hours. His fears drove him to his knees. He knelt beside the bed determined to pray, no matter how great the struggle. But each time he tried to lift his *mamm* and her health before the Lord, the specter of his past—his failures, his rebellion, his sins—stood in the way, blocking his petitions.

Finally, he broke down and confessed. Every detail,

every wrongdoing, every sin stemmed from his rebellion. He'd turned his back on God, railed against Him, refused to accept His will after *Dat*'s death. As time passed, he'd become angrier and hardened his heart.

God, forgive me, he cried silently. The burdens weighing him down lifted, and his heart felt lighter, but he had one more roadblock to peace. After wrestling internally, he finally gave in completely. *Not my will, but Yours, Lord.*

As soon as those words left his lips, his spirit soared. He'd accept God's plan for his life, even if it meant not marrying Rebecca or losing *Mamm*.

He had one more thing to do tonight. Paul had said to use anything in the apartment, so Abner went to the desk in the kitchen alcove and took out a sheet of paper and an envelope. Then he sat down and composed a letter. After he folded it and inserted it into the envelope, he sealed and addressed it. Tomorrow he'd get a stamp and drop it in the mail. His heart assured him he'd made the right decision.

The first rays of dawn streaming through the window touched Abner's face, and before he opened his eyes, he basked in a sense of rightness. His life had been renewed. Paul had spoken of the same feeling. The cleanness and freshness of a forgiven life. And the knowledge that God was now in control.

After whispering a brief prayer of thanksgiving, Abner slipped from his bed to call the clinic. He hung up the phone rejoicing.

Although they could not assure him *Mamm* would recover, she had made it through the night. Abner made an appointment to see the doctor as soon as she came in, and he planned to be at the clinic the minute it opened. He'd have to skip work in the morning, but after his decision last night, that might not be a problem.

Abner made sure his brothers woke and dressed earlier than usual. He needed to waylay Paul and talk to him before it was time to leave for the studio. They knocked at the other apartment door, and Rebecca let them in. She searched his face for any sign of news.

He answered the unspoken question. "*Mamm* made it through the night. They couldn't give me details of her condition over the phone, so I'm going over there this morning."

"That's wonderful," Rebecca said. "I'll be praying she continues to improve."

Esther, who was cooking in the kitchen, chimed in, "Thanks be to God. He is good."

Once Abner would have winced at that statement, but today he agreed. Rebecca, who must have been expecting his usual sour look, raised her eyebrows. Evidently, she'd noticed something was different. Rather than telling her about last night, he wanted her to see the changes in his life, to demonstrate that his commitment to God was real.

When Paul arrived bearing a huge bakery box of pastries, Abner asked him to come to the other apartment. Paul sighed and tore his gaze from Esther, who'd come out of the kitchen to take the box from him. He trailed Abner down the hall and into the living room.

Abner motioned him to a chair and sat across from him. "I got right with God last night."

A huge smile spread across Paul's face. "That's great, man!"

Yes, it was, but it might not be so great for Paul when he found out Abner's plan. "I want to spend today with my *mamm*. She made it through the night, but we have no guarantee how long she'll be with us."

"I understand. Herman will rage, but he'll get over it. Take whatever time you need."

"The thing is"—Abner swallowed hard—"after last night, I don't feel right coming back at all. I shouldn't have done that screen test, and I never should have agreed to work for you."

"I understand, but that'll put the studio in a bind."

"I know," Abner said. "I just don't feel I can honor God and continue to work in that atmosphere." And after what had happened with Brooklyn, he wanted to stay as far away from her as he could.

Paul tapped a finger against his lip. "I can't ask you to do something that goes against your conscience. We'll have to figure out how to handle the rest of the training."

"Thank you. I appreciate it. Also, we'll need to pay you if we stay in these apartments."

"Don't worry about it." Paul waved a hand as if to dismiss the cost as minimal.

"I wouldn't feel right doing that. How much are they a month?"

When Paul told him the cost, Abner gulped. He totaled the price of both apartments for two months, and his head spun. If he had that kind of money, he could pay off a year of the mortgage at the farm.

"I—I had no idea they were that much. We'll have

to move out immediately. Rebecca and Esther can take the boys home. I'll find a small place where I can stay to be near *Mamm*."

"Just stay here. The company pays the rent whether the apartments are empty or occupied. We use them for visiting actors or investors. Herman has no one lined up for the next few months while we're working on this show."

Abner refused to accept charity. He'd have to find a way to take care of this. But right now, he needed to see *Mamm*.

Paul glanced at his watch. "If you want to get to the hospital when visiting hours begin, we should leave in the next ten minutes."

Abner picked up the letter. "I'd like to mail this today, if possible."

"Give it to me. I'll see that it gets sent." Paul refused the dollar Abner held out for the stamp. "Consider it part of your pay."

One more thing they'd have to discuss. With leaving before the job was completed, they'd have to dock his pay. And what would he do for work if he stayed here in New York with *Mamm*?

After a hurried breakfast, everyone piled into the limo and headed to the hospital. Abner debated going alone, but he wanted his brothers to have some time with *Mamm* in case…

Rebecca studied Abner, trying to decide why he seemed so different. Instead of the agitation he'd displayed last night, he gave off an air of calmness and, perhaps, acceptance. Maybe her prayers that he'd yield to God's will had affected him.

He'd also subdued his rebellious streak. That burning fire, that challenging of authority, had once been an attraction. Now she desired quiet, inner strength.

Beside her, Paul slid an envelope into the upper pocket of his overcoat. Rebecca hadn't meant to pry, but she couldn't help noticing the letter was addressed to Bishop Troyer. That piqued her curiosity. Why would Paul be writing to the head of their Amish community?

With the envelope in place, Paul lifted his fingers, revealing the return address—Abner's address. Abner was writing to the bishop? Perhaps he was only keeping the community informed about his *mamm*'s condition. But a little seed of hope sprouted in her heart.

After they arrived at the clinic, Rebecca and Esther settled the boys in the waiting room, while Abner checked on his *mamm*'s status. With a bleak look in his eyes, he returned.

"She's still unresponsive. I'm meeting with the doctor in a few minutes. They requested no more than two people in the room at a time."

Before Abner pivoted, Rebecca noticed his lips moving. Was he praying? She bowed her head and offered a prayer for him as well as his *mamm*.

She gathered the boys around her and got down to their level so she could look into their eyes. "Your *mamm* is still feeling very sick, so she might be too tired to open her eyes, but you can talk to her softly."

Rebecca and Esther took turns taking one boy at a time in to see Adah. The boys sat quietly or told their *mamm* about the sights they'd observed from the apartment window. Rebecca took Philip in last.

He tiptoed to the bed. *"Mamm?"* When she didn't answer, he repeated her name again and jostled her arm.

Rebecca set her hands on his shoulders and moved him out of touching distance.

"She's not listening to me."

Turning him to face her, Rebecca squatted down to his level. "I know it's hard, but your *mamm* can't answer right now. Remember I said to talk to her in a quiet voice?"

He nodded. "But I want her to talk back." His whine turned into a wail, and Rebecca cuddled him close.

"Shh," she whispered as she rubbed his back and hurried for the door. She'd take him out into the hallway to comfort him.

The door flew open, and she barreled right into Abner's chest. Abner wrapped his arms around her to steady her. The collision startled Philip into silence.

Rebecca's heart throbbed in an unsteady rhythm as Abner gazed into her eyes. She was grateful Philip was between them, or she'd have been tempted to melt against Abner's chest.

Abner closed his eyes and tried to draw a breath into his constricted chest. Bumping into Philip had knocked some of the air from his lungs. But the tenderness in Rebecca's eyes and the softness of her forearms against his arms left him gasping. He should let go, but after the doctor's bad news, he desperately needed comfort.

"What did the doctor say?" Rebecca whispered.

Keeping his arms around her, he drew her into the

hall and let the door swing shut. He flicked his eyes in Philip's direction. "The prognosis is not good."

"I'm so sorry."

Philip looked from one to the other. "What's prog-no-tis? I want to see *Mamm*."

Before his brother's request increased to a yell, Abner released Rebecca and lifted Philip from her arms.

"I'll take him in to see *Mamm*. Thanks for taking care of the boys."

Rebecca laid a hand on his arm. "I'll be praying."

The warmth of her hand heated his arm through the cotton sleeve and set his blood on fire. If he hadn't been carrying Philip, he could never have resisted the temptation to enfold her in his arms. He managed to choke out, *"Danke."*

He forced himself to turn away and enter the room. "You need to be very quiet," he cautioned Philip.

"I know," his brother answered, his face sober. "Rebecca told me."

Abner sat on the chair beside the bed with Philip on his lap. He reached out and laid one hand on *Mamm*'s.

"I want to hold her hand too."

Abner shot him a warning look to remind him to keep his voice down. Then he scooted the chair as close to the bed as he could. *"Mamm* can't hold hands right now, but you can put your hand over hers like this." Philip leaned over and followed his lead. Then Abner placed his hand atop his brother's.

Philip began a long, rambling story.

Mamm's heart monitor blipped, drawing a higher point than before.

Abner stood and rushed for the door. "We can save

the rest for another time." He yanked on the knob and came face to face with Rebecca. If he'd been hooked up to a heart monitor, his blips would have been off the charts.

"I thought you might want some time alone with your *mamm*," she said, "so I'll take Philip." She reached for his brother, and their hands brushed.

"I appreciate it," he managed to say. Then he stood in the doorway staring until the elevator doors closed behind her.

Back in the room, he settled into the chair. The change in *Mamm*'s heart rate when Philip spoke convinced Abner she was listening.

First he told her a little about himself and the boys, then he moved on to his most important news. He described his wrestling and eventual surrender to God. "I've turned my life over to the Lord, and I'll be joining the church." He'd promised Rebecca he'd join the church, but this time he'd do it because of a heartfelt commitment rather than to please the woman he wanted to marry.

Mamm's eyes fluttered open. "I'm…glad…" The breathy sounds barely formed words.

Abner rejoiced. Even if he lost *Mamm*, at least she knew his heart was right with God.

"I'll be sure the boys are raised right," he assured her. "But we all need you, so I'm praying you'll be healed."

"…God's…will."

"Yes, I'll accept whatever happens as God's will." It would be hard, but now at least he'd have God's comfort. Something he'd sorely needed but refused to acknowledge after *Dat*'s death.

Mamm's eyes slid closed. He didn't want to overtax her, so he patted her hand. "I'll let you rest now."

He'd almost reached the door when her whisper reached him. "Re...becca?"

Abner turned. "You want me to send her in?"

Mamm's barely perceptible nod showed he'd guessed right.

Rebecca and Esther were discussing what to do about lunch when Abner entered.

"*Mamm* would like to see you," he said.

"Me?" When Abner nodded, Rebecca asked, "How do you know? Is she awake and talking?"

"She said a few words."

"That's *wunderbar*."

He nodded. "At least I got to tell her something important, but you might want to hurry. She's very tired."

Rebecca rushed to the room. "Adah?" she said as she approached the bed. "It's Rebecca. I'm here."

No answer. *Please, Lord, help her to be all right.*

After Rebecca opened her eyes, the sheet stirred ever so slightly. Adah was still breathing. Rebecca reached out to hold the callused, wrinkled hand atop the sheet. "Abner said you wanted me."

Adah's eyelids fluttered partway open. "Take... care...of...my...boys." Each word was an effort.

Rebecca had agreed to this before, but Adah hadn't been so close to death. Could she really care for Adah's children? Mothering four boys meant giving up her own desires and putting their needs first. Was she ready to take on that responsibility?

Abner's *mamm* needed reassurance, but Rebecca had

to be certain about making this commitment. Once she gave her word, she intended to keep it. *God, if this is Your will, please give me the strength.*

After she raised her head, she met Adah's eyes. "I will. I'll do my best to care for the boys."

Despite the exhaustion on her face, Adah scrutinized Rebecca as if peering into her soul. "All...of...them?"

Adah meant all five of her boys, not only the younger ones. She meant Abner too.

Rebecca swallowed hard. She had no idea what making this vow would mean, but she would do her best. "I promise."

Adah closed her eyes with the soft sigh of a soul at peace.

Chapter Twenty

When Abner reached the lobby, his brothers sat silent, their hands in their laps, swinging their legs back and forth. All their expressions were somber. All except Philip, who had a gleam in his eye that appeared mischievous. Esther narrowed her eyes and moved to the edge of her chair as if readying for a chase.

"Philip." Abner kept his tone sharp, and his brother jumped.

After one glance at his older brother's stern face, Philip sighed, and his shoulders slumped.

Abner pulled his cell phone out of his pocket to check the time. *Ach*, all those missed calls. It dawned on him he'd turned off his phone the other day and forgotten to turn it back on. Every single one of them was from Herman. Abner would have to call him back, but the thought filled him with dread. Herman would be furious.

Abner strode to the glassed-in entryway to have some privacy. He hit the callback button and waited till Herman answered. Abner's *hello* came out shaky.

"What's this Paul tells me about you not coming back?" Herman griped. "Some fool thing about finding God?"

"That's right." About this Abner could be firm. He'd stand by his convictions.

"We had a deal. You can't just back out."

"I'm really sorry. I never should have agreed to do something that went against my principles."

"Principles-schminciples. You've had time off to spend with your mother. Now get back over here after lunch. I'm sending the limo for you."

A muffled noise sounded in the background, then some squawking. An unintelligible conversation, followed by a long, drawn-out sigh.

"Never mind. Paul says he already sent a limo to pick everyone up and drop them at the apartment for the lunch he's having delivered. Grab your meal and come straight here."

"I'm afraid I can't do that."

Abner could picture Herman's red face as he screamed, "I'll dock your salary. You won't see one penny of your pay."

"I understand," Abner said. "If I'm not fulfilling my contract, I don't deserve to be paid."

"I mean all of it. That's not the only thing I'll do. You'd better be here by one or else."

Or else Herman would broadcast the video. Sick inside, Abner struggled to keep his voice calm. "I'm still at the hospital, but I'll call you back later with my answer."

"It had better be *yes*," Herman snapped. The phone clicked off.

Abner sank into the nearest chair. What was he going to do now?

"Abner?" Rebecca had entered the waiting room and was staring at him, her brow wrinkled in concern. "What's wrong?"

The time had come for him to confess. But not here. Not now.

"Can I talk to you when we get back?" he asked.

"Of course."

For the first time, he noticed her paleness. "Are you all right?" He leaped to his feet. "Is *Mamm*…"

"She's sleeping."

The tightness in his chest eased. "I'll go in to see her briefly, but then we should take the boys home."

He only had time to give *Mamm*'s hand a light squeeze and tell her he'd return that evening before Esther tapped on the door to tell him the limo had arrived.

The food delivery arrived soon after they reached the apartment, and Abner asked Rebecca to unlock the connecting door so they could talk privately. Esther and the boys could act as chaperones because they could see into his apartment from the dining room table, but they couldn't hear the discussion.

Once they sat down, Abner struggled with how to start. "I promised myself I'd never lie to you again after I tricked you into the filming, but I've been keeping something from you."

Rebecca's heart clenched. She knew what was coming. He'd tell her he was in love with that painted-up actress. She bit her lower lip to keep from crying.

Abner hung his head and stared down at the floor. "I took this job because Herman blackmailed me."

Her head jerked up. "Blackmailed?"

"He threatened to air the film he has of us if I didn't help him. I refused to act, but I agreed to teach the actors."

Rebecca shook her head. "That's impossible. He claimed he destroyed it."

"He lied."

"But—but that's…" She couldn't find words to describe how violated she felt.

"Yes, it's unfair, cruel, and a lot of other things. But that's why I agreed to help him with this show. He promised he'd really destroy the tape this time."

"How can you trust him to do what he says?"

"I've been worried about that, but once he's shot the show, he'll have no need to use our clip. I hope Paul can convince him to delete it."

Rebecca wasn't convinced, and Abner's glum expression told her it wasn't likely his plan would succeed. She hadn't trusted either of those two men from the moment she met them. Paul seemed to have changed somewhat, but still—

Abner broke into her thoughts. "Last night changed everything for me." He told Rebecca about spending the night on his knees and getting right with the Lord. "And so, I don't feel I should go back to the studio. Except Herman called when we were at the hospital and threatened to air the clip if I don't come in."

Rebecca wanted to tell him to defy Herman, but that would mean embarrassment and shame. Not only for her, but for her family. As the bishop's daughter, she should have set a better example. When the community found out what she'd done, they'd be shocked. So would the *Englischers* who knew her family. But she'd promised Adah to take care of *all* her sons. This would be her first opportunity.

"Abner," she said at last, "I support your decision to quit." Visions of that painted actress flitted through her mind. Maybe she'd also be keeping him away from another temptation.

"But they still have the film, and Herman will follow up on his threat."

"What we did was wrong, and perhaps this is fitting punishment. It will keep me humble." A lesson she needed to learn. "More important is that I don't want you to go against your conscience."

Hadn't he said almost the exact same words to Zander? He couldn't believe Rebecca was willing to sacrifice her reputation. "Are you sure?"

"Very sure." The firmness of her tone left little doubt she meant it.

"Rebecca, I wish I could go back and erase the past. When I think of what I've done, it makes me sick. I'm the one who did wrong. It isn't fair for you to suffer."

Rebecca looked him straight in the eye. "Although I didn't know we were being filmed, I defied my parents and sneaked out with you. I also used my friend Sarah as an excuse to lie about my whereabouts, so I'm not innocent."

"Still, it doesn't seem right." Abner wished there were a way he could take the full blame. She didn't deserve the exposure or humiliation.

Gazing off into space, Rebecca mused, "I wonder if God uses our rebellion too."

Abner wasn't sure he heard her right. "You think God wants us to rebel?"

Rebecca shook her head. "No, I'm sure he doesn't, but don't you think He can even use the things we do wrong?"

Abner had never thought about that before. Suppose, though, instead of rebelling, he'd submitted to God's will? What might have happened then? He'd have joined the church when the time came, but he'd never have realized how far he could fall, so he'd never have known the extent of God's forgiveness.

"You know," Abner said, "the greatest good from my rebellion is experiencing the depth of God's mercy. I would never have appreciated His forgiveness the way I do now. It's also made me less judgmental. I can't be critical of others, knowing what I've done."

"I feel the same way." Then she lowered her eyes. "I hope you won't think I was prying, but Paul had a letter in his pocket addressed to the bishop. It had your return address."

Abner had been hoping to keep that a secret. He'd wanted to surprise her when he showed up for baptismal classes, but he was done with evading the truth. Besides, this was one secret he wanted to share. "I told the bishop I planned to start classes this spring."

"Oh, Abner." Rebecca's face glowed as she flashed her brilliant smile. A smile meant only for him. A smile that showed she'd forgiven him. A smile that promised a special future together.

He longed to gather her into his arms, to cradle her softness against his chest, but he fought the temptation. This time he'd do everything right.

Rebecca's heart overflowed with joy over Abner's decision. Ever since she'd gotten right with the Lord, she'd prayed that Abner would turn his life over to God and commit to joining the church. Instead he'd strayed further from God, and Rebecca had feared his mother's death would drive him away completely. Yet, this tragedy had brought him closer to the Lord.

She whispered a prayer of thanksgiving, along with a request for a miracle for Adah.

Abner's cell phone buzzed, and Rebecca jumped. Only three people might be calling him—Herman, Paul, or the hospital. She rose to give him privacy, but Abner held out a hand, imploring her to stay.

She waited while he murmured a greeting and held the phone to his ear. The voice on the other end was too quiet for Rebecca to distinguish words, but the lack of screaming from the receiver made it clear the caller was not Herman.

After listening for a long while, Abner frowned. "I see." But he seemed rather dazed as the voice droned on. "Yes, we did agree to that." After another long pause, he added, "Whatever you think is best."

From his conversation, it could be Paul or the hospital. His responses gave nothing away. Rebecca shot him a questioning glance, and he motioned for her to wait. She fidgeted until he thanked the caller and hung up.

He exhaled a long breath and bowed his head, rubbing his forehead.

"Is something wrong?" Rebecca asked. She longed to reach out to comfort him, but he'd made no move to touch her after his confession. Perhaps accepting God's will meant he no longer planned to court her.

"That was the hospital. They reminded me that *Mamm*'s consent form allowed for experimental measures to counteract the treatment. I didn't really understand it, but they plan to try something new. It's risky, but they believe it will help."

Rebecca reached for his hand. "Let's pray it'll work."

Abner squeezed her hand as they both closed their eyes and sent up silent petitions. Once they lifted their heads, Abner slid his hand from hers, and Rebecca missed the warmth and connection.

"I wish we could go back to the hospital to be with her, but they asked us to stay away today and tomorrow, especially the boys. They're worried about her picking up germs during this treatment because she'll be in a fragile state." He lifted anguished eyes to her face. "What if she doesn't make it? If I never get a chance to say good-bye?"

Rebecca pleated tiny fan folds in the fabric of her apron skirt to keep her hands occupied. Her heart ached for him, and she longed to comfort him. He'd avoided her touch, though, so she wouldn't chance reaching out again.

The only way she could help was through her words. "We just prayed for God's healing. We have to trust He knows best."

If God could change two rebellious souls like Abner

and her, surely he could heal Adah. But what if healing wasn't in His plans?

If that were the case, Rebecca had promised she'd care for the boys, yet she and Abner couldn't marry until they joined the church. How would she keep her promise?

All the questions running through her mind were about her and how she'd cope. She needed to concentrate on Abner. Losing his *mamm* would be devastating for him and the boys. He'd need help and support.

She turned to him. "I pray God will work a miracle. I want you to know, though, that whatever happens, I'll be there to help."

Abner's eyes filled with gratitude. "Your support means more to me than you'll ever know." The unspoken message in his gaze revealed his love.

When they'd first started dating, Abner had been self-absorbed, and so had she. Turning his life over to God had changed him deeply on the inside. A change she could read in his expression. Now his only concern seemed to be for others rather than himself.

He proved it by asking, "How will I ever handle caring for the boys? I'm not the spiritual leader *Mamm* is for our family. I can't lead by example. All I can tell them is not to make my mistakes."

"We're both examples of God's grace."

"That's for sure and certain. At least as far as I'm concerned."

Rebecca wanted to protest. She'd also been rebellious. If only she could go back and fix the past and right all her wrongs. The only comfort she had now was that if she'd been different and been obedient to God, she and Abner never would have dated. Once again, she wondered if their disobedience had served a purpose—to teach them a lesson and bring them face to face with God's forgiveness.

Abner couldn't keep his eyes off Rebecca. She had a glow around her that appeared almost heavenly. From the serenity of her expression, he guessed she was thinking of spiritual things. Once that would have bothered him. Now that his life had been turned around, he found it enhanced her attraction.

The doorbell rang, and Abner's chest constricted. What if Herman had sent the limo to pick him up? Or worse yet, what if Herman had decided to come in person? Picturing that explosion, he dragged his feet heading to the door.

Esther answered before he reached the living room. The saccharine sweetness in her voice made it clear who was at the door.

Abner picked up his pace, although he was sure he wouldn't like the news—or ultimatum—Paul intended to deliver.

"Why don't we go into the other apartment so we can talk privately?" Paul suggested.

When Abner and Paul entered, Rebecca scurried out of the apartment. Abner wished he could ask her to stay, but he wasn't sure he wanted her to hear what Paul had to say.

Paul closed the apartment door and took the chair opposite Abner. "I hate to be the bearer of bad news, but Herman is livid. I've talked him out of suing you, but he's determined to make you pay."

Abner didn't blame him. He'd agreed to help with the show. "Would it be all right if I recorded the script so the actors still could hear my words?"

"That might help," Paul said, but he didn't sound too certain.

"I won't charge him anything for what I've done so far. Maybe he can use that money to hire someone else."

Paul blew out a breath. "How's your mom?"

Abner blinked at the abrupt change of subject. *"Mamm?"* A heavy weight crushed his chest, forcing all the air out of his lungs. He fought to drag in a breath. "She's, well, not very good right now. They're trying something experimental, but we can't visit her because she's too fragile. The doctor doesn't want any germs."

"I was afraid of that." Paul set his hands on his knees and leaned forward. "Herman wants you out of the apartments today."

"Today? We don't have train tickets. We haven't packed. And I can't leave *Mamm* alone in New York."

"That's what I told him. How long do you think you'll need to stay?"

"I—I'm not sure. It could be a few months, or"—he squeezed his eyes shut—"it could be much sooner, if she doesn't recover from this…"

"I understand." The compassion in Paul's eyes showed he truly did understand and care. "So, here's what I negotiated. You can stay here for up to two months. I hope and pray your mother will be well enough to go home by then."

"Danke."

Paul held up a hand. "You might not thank me when

you hear the terms. I convinced Herman he needed to pay you for the work you've done, but…"

That was great, wasn't it? Yet, at the way Paul drew the last word out so long, Abner's stomach dropped.

"Here's the deal, man." Paul didn't meet Abner's eyes. "Herman plans to keep all your pay to cover the cost of the apartment rents. He wanted to charge you full market value for the time you were here. I nixed that. The apartments were part of your pay, but starting from today, the rental will be charged against your salary."

"I see." With how much the apartments cost, Abner's pay wouldn't last long.

"I hate to do this, but Herman has the final say on all company decisions. He did insist I give you one final offer. It goes against my conscience, but I agreed to tell you the terms. Herman's willing to forgive everything, let you stay here as long as you like, pay your full salary, and destroy the tape, if…"

"If I stay?" Abner guessed, and Paul nodded.

Blackmail seemed to be Herman's specialty. Not destroying the tape affected Rebecca too, so Abner needed to be sure his answer reflected both of their preferences. From their earlier conversation, he could guess her answer, but he wanted to reconfirm it. "Could I discuss this with Rebecca before I make a final decision?"

"Of course." Paul stood. "I'm sure you'd like privacy. Why don't I go into the other apartment?"

So you can spend time with Esther. That bothered Abner, but what could he say except *yes*?

When Rebecca arrived, Abner recapped what Paul

had told him. "I'm so sorry," he said. "This is all my fault."

Rebecca reached for his hand. "We're in this together. You've made the right decision, and I'm ready to face the consequences."

"Thank you." He was grateful for her support, but doing the right thing would be rough.

Losing his pay meant he wouldn't be able to afford to marry Rebecca even after they joined the church. It wouldn't be fair to court her until he found a job and had a steady paycheck. A paycheck that would cover all the household bills and support his brothers and a wife. If *Mamm* didn't make it, was it fair to ask Rebecca to care for four young boys?

Chapter Twenty-One

The two days dragged by for all of them. Paul stopped by several times to give them updates on Herman's temper tantrums and to assure them he'd been doing his best to calm the outbursts. Negotiations didn't seem to be going well because Herman wanted to back out of the apartment deal, but Paul remained determined to work everything out. He also popped in with meals and snacks, or to ask for updates on Abner's *mamm*.

"You could have called about that," Abner said pointedly.

Paul's face reddened. "I suppose I could, but I was in the area."

They all knew his real reason for stopping by, and it concerned Abner.

Right now, though, his main focus was on *Mamm*. She'd made it through three days of life-saving measures. According to the clinic updates, she'd stabilized that evening but remained quite weak.

"Call tomorrow," the doctor told him. "If she remains stable overnight, we may allow visitors."

Abner tossed and turned all night, praying for *Mamm* and for his future with Rebecca. He slipped out of bed at dawn and continued sending petitions up to heaven until he could call the hospital at eight.

"The adults can visit this morning," the doctor said, "but limit it to ten minutes each. I'd prefer the children wait until tomorrow."

In much happier spirits, Abner headed to the other apartment for breakfast. "*Mamm*'s doing much better," he announced with a smile.

His brothers cheered. Rebecca and Esther both murmured, "Praise the Lord."

"Only adults can see *Mamm* today, though."

"I can stay here with the boys," Esther offered but then looked at Rebecca. "If they can take a little time off their studies, that is. I know Adah wanted to see you last time."

Rebecca turned to Abner. "Would that be all right?" At his nod, she said, "I'll start their lessons when I return."

As much as Abner wanted to spend time alone with Rebecca, Paul's frequent visits worried him. Rather than avoiding the *Englischer*, Esther seemed to welcome his company. And his attention.

"Why don't we take the boys along, and you can help us watch them?" Abner said to Esther. "That way Rebecca can do some teaching in the limo and while they wait." *And protect you from being alone with Paul.*

With Rebecca pressed close to his side in the limo, Abner tried to tamp down his reaction to her by taking deep breaths and blowing out long, silent exhales, but they came out as sighs.

"Are you all right?" she asked.

Abner couldn't lie. "I'm concerned about *Mamm*, but being near you like this…"

Her soft *I know* made it even harder. Abner had no idea how he'd be able to spend time with her and not touch her. He was grateful when they arrived at the hospital.

While Rebecca and Esther settled all the children in the waiting room, Abner went alone to *Mamm*'s room. He eased the door open, sat beside the bed, and took her hand. At first she didn't stir. At least today her chest rose and fell in even, deep breaths, and the heart monitor recorded stronger peaks.

Bowing his head, he whispered a prayer of thanksgiving. When he lifted his head, *Mamm*'s gaze was fixed on him. Her lips curved into a tired smile.

"I wondered if I'd dreamed what you told me the other day. I'm so glad to see it's real."

"It's definitely real."

She lifted her head from the pillow and studied him. "And you're joining the church?"

"Yes, Rebecca and I will both start baptismal classes in May."

"That's *wunderbar*." *Mamm* sank back against the pillow and closed her eyes. "I hope I'll be around to see that."

Abner hoped so too. "I'm sure you will be. The doctor said all your vitals are back to where they were when you arrived. You've passed the crisis point." *One of them at least. And you didn't become another fatality in the study. Thank God!*

"Now I have to start the treatment again."

"I know. They've adjusted some things so it will be more successful."

Mamm gripped his hand. "But if it's not, encourage your brothers to stay in the faith."

"I will, *Mamm*, but you'll have plenty of time to make sure of that." *He prayed he spoke the truth.*

"How is she?" Rebecca asked when Abner returned to the lobby.

"Tired, but she looks so much better."

"That's great. Do you think she'll want to see me?"

"I'm sure she will. I reassured her I'd be joining the church, which made her very happy."

The enthusiasm in his voice erased all of Rebecca's worries about his faith. He truly had changed. She headed up to Adah's room with a wide grin and a bounce in her steps. But outside the door, she sobered. Bowing her head, she prayed God would work a miracle.

"I was hoping you'd come," Adah said when Rebecca pushed open the door.

"I won't stay long, because I'm sure you're tired," Rebecca told her. "It's great that you're recovering."

"Only from one thing, dear. Not from the cancer yet."

"I'm praying the treatments will work too." Rebecca lowered herself into the chair.

"If the Good Lord wills."

Rebecca nodded. She hoped Adah would be around to see her boys grow up.

"God has answered one of my prayers." Adah's eyes sparkled. "I spent many hours on my knees begging God to touch Abner's soul. And also yours."

Rebecca cringed, remembering all the heartache

their rebellion had caused. They'd never given a thought to how many people they were hurting.

Adah reached over and patted Rebecca's hand. "I didn't say that to make you feel guilty. I'm just so thrilled Abner has surrendered his life to God. Once you both join the church, the two of you can marry."

"Yes, we can." Rebecca's heart leaped at the promise of their future together. Only a short while ago, that future had been in doubt.

"Tell my boys I love them." Adah closed her eyes. "I can rest easy now, knowing you've promised to take care of all of them, including Abner."

"I'll do my best," Rebecca whispered as she rose. That was one promise she intended to keep.

Abner shivered in the cold as he stood in the vestibule to update Paul. Although Paul seemed pleased to hear about *Mamm*'s recovery, he also questioned when they'd be returning to the apartment.

Abner sighed inwardly. "I'm not sure yet. It depends on Rebecca—"

Her reflection wavered in the glass in front of him, and he lost track of what he was saying. He spun around to watch her enter the lobby and kneel to speak to his brothers. They leaned closer to her, and after she finished talking, she gave each one a hug. Such a simple, heartfelt act, but it set Abner's pulse on fire.

"You there?" Paul's voice on the phone startled Abner.

He'd forgotten he hadn't finished their conversation. "Um, *jah*."

That wasn't the complete truth. He was too engrossed

in watching Rebecca to pay attention to Paul's nattering. Abner did tune back in when Paul announced he'd bring them dinner.

"You don't need to do that. You've done enough already, especially after I quit on the project." He had to find a way to discourage Paul from visiting.

"It's no problem. I'll be in that area anyway." Before Abner could protest again, Paul said, "Oops, gotta go. Herman's yelling, and the star's threatening to walk off the set." He hung up.

Abner stood there holding the dead phone. At the moment, Esther was the least of his worries. With his attraction to Rebecca deepening every day, waiting until the fall to court her seemed unbearable. If he could even do it then. What seemed even more impossible was finding a way to support her and his family.

Rebecca spied him through the glass, and her face lit up, flooding his heart with excitement. She'd supported him through everything despite what he'd done. Her actions provided a demonstration here on earth of God's mercy and love. Abner didn't deserve her forgiveness— or the Lord's—but he was deeply grateful for both.

Rebecca tried to hide her frown when Paul showed up at suppertime again. From the worried look on Abner's face, he had the same misgivings. Esther, however, exuded enthusiasm.

Abner pulled Rebecca aside after Paul left that evening. "I'm worried about Paul and Esther."

"I am too," she whispered. "I don't think she'd leave the church or do anything foolish. Still, Paul can be quite charming, so—"

Abner frowned. "*You* think he's charming?"

She laughed and touched his arm. "I meant toward Esther." Her cheeks flushed pink as she added, "You know I've only ever had eyes for one man."

The warmth of Abner's skin radiated through her palm and set Rebecca's pulse pounding. She longed for him to pull her close and wrap her in an embrace. The burning intensity in his eyes revealed he wished for the same, but he was exercising powerful self-control.

She respected his decision not to date until they were with the church to begin courting. With a deep sigh, she let her hand drop to her side. Waiting all that time would be excruciating. She whispered a prayer for God's strength to get them through the long months ahead.

Eight months later...

Scarlet, russet, and maize leaves floated from the sky to blanket the ground under Rebecca's feet as she crossed the lawn with her family to enter Abner's house for church. Today she—and Abner!—would be joining the church. To do it here in his home with his *mamm* well enough to witness their special day meant so much to all of them. The beauty of the world around them matched the joy in Rebecca's heart.

Her brother Jakob pushed *Dat*'s wheelchair up the sidewalk, and Rebecca walked beside him. *Mamm*, her face stretched into a broad grin, stayed at his other side. People swarmed over to welcome their former bishop.

"It's so good to see you here today," a man said.

Dat's answer was garbled, but Rebecca understood

his words. "*Danke*…I…want…to…be…here…for…
my…daughter's…baptism."

Both her parents had wondered if this day would
ever come, so they were thrilled. Until last winter, even
Rebecca herself had viewed her future in the church as
clouded with doubt. Today, though, all uncertainty had
disappeared, and she was ready to make a spiritual commitment to God and to her community. She was grateful to have her family, especially *Dat*, who was rarely
able to leave the house since he'd had his second stroke,
here to witness her baptism. And her heart overflowed
with thanksgiving because Abner would be joining her
in making this lifelong commitment.

Adah met them at the door. "Abner is out in the barn,
helping with the horses." She beamed at Rebecca. "I'm
so happy you and Abner will be joining the church this
morning. God has been so good, hasn't He?"

"*Jah*… He…has," her *dat* gurgled. Although only
one side of his mouth lifted into a smile, his eyes shone
with delight.

Rebecca had struggled with rebellion for so long,
she'd never expected to see her parents express happi-
ness over her life choices. Jakob had always been held
up as a shining example. She'd always fallen short of
their expectations. But today they were pleased.

Jakob gave her a special smile, but then glanced
around for Sarah, the love of his life.

"Sarah's helping in the kitchen," Adah told him.

His disappointment was obvious, but he pushed *Dat*'s
wheelchair to the room where the men were gathering.
Adah ushered them to the kitchen, where they joined
the women.

Before they entered, Adah set a hand on Rebecca's arm and whispered, "*Danke* for all your help."

Earlier in the week, Rebecca had helped her scrub the house, bake snitz pies, and prepare peanut butter spread and spicy pretzels. When the church truck arrived, she and Adah had set dishes and silverware on the serving tables while Abner and his brothers unloaded the backless benches. Abner's smile widened every time he passed her, and the look in his eyes filled her with longing.

"I was happy to help," Rebecca said. And particularly happy to spend so much time around Abner.

"We have so much to be grateful for," Adah replied.

Rebecca couldn't agree more. What a blessing to see Adah almost back to her old self. Last week they'd been assured the cancer was in remission. So they were all rejoicing about that victory.

The bishop's wife urged everyone to head to the women's benches. Rebecca joined the other candidates for baptism in the front row. She looked over to meet Abner's eyes. His special smile warmed her whole body.

Rebecca had never dreamed this day would come. She and the man she loved would be united in faith and community. After that…

Her thoughts were interrupted as the candidates rose to file out to meet with the bishop. The congregation sang as she and the others headed to the basement for their final preparations for baptism.

When the bishop warned anyone who was uncertain about making this promise for life to reconsider and turn back now, Rebecca had no doubt she'd made the right choice. Abner hadn't changed his mind, had he? She sneaked a glance at him.

His eyes shining, he'd focused his full attention on the bishop. Her heart singing, Rebecca did the same.

When they returned to the service, the bishop began his sermon about Philip and the Ethiopian, one Rebecca had heard every other year during baptismal services. But this time the ringing words—"What doth hinder me to be baptized?"—held an extra-special meaning for her.

When they reached the part for their participation, Rebecca's heart overflowed as she began her commitment with the words "I believe that Jesus Christ is the Son of God." And as she knelt and the bishop held his hands over her head, water trickled down onto her head confirming outwardly the promise she'd made in her heart.

Then the bishop's wife helped her to her feet and greeted her with a holy kiss, and Rebecca's spirit soared. She was now with the church.

Seated in his wheelchair at the front of the men's side, *Dat*'s eyes glistened with tears as he gazed first at her and then at Abner. Rebecca knew *Dat* had spent many years praying she and Abner would give up their wayward ways. Today, his prayers had been answered. Rebecca had also spent months praying for Abner, so this day held special meaning for each one of them.

For the first time, Rebecca scanned the congregation. She stopped in shock. *Paul. What is he doing here?* His lips quirked into a smile when he caught her staring.

After the service, the men changed the benches into

tables, and they ate first. As Rebecca replenished the homemade bread, Paul stood in line with Abner.

"I'd like to talk to both of you once all this is over." Paul waved a hand at the table laden with food.

Rebecca nodded, flashed Abner a special smile, and scurried off, but inside worry churned her stomach. What did Paul want? He hadn't come to talk Abner into returning to New York, had he? Abner had given up every penny of his pay in exchange for staying in the apartment. But what if Herman demanded more? And Herman still owned the video, which, despite Paul's pleading, he'd refused to destroy. Suppose Paul had come to warn them Herman planned to air that footage?

Rebecca was too jittery to stay still. She flitted around the kitchen, bouncing from job to job.

"Are you all right?" Adah asked as Rebecca's trembling hands splashed red beet juice onto the counter rather than into the serving bowl.

Rather than answering her question, Rebecca responded with one of her own. "Did you know Paul was here?"

Adah nodded. "He dropped by last night, and Abner invited him to church today. He contacted the bishop to be sure it was all right, and once the bishop heard about Paul's change of heart, he agreed to let him attend your baptism."

But Adah had no idea why Paul wanted to attend. And with each passing minute, Rebecca's anxiety increased until it was unbearable. *Mamm* always said worry meant you weren't trusting God for the outcome, so Rebecca whispered a prayer to accept His will, even if it meant separating her and Abner.

* * *

Abner stared after Rebecca until she disappeared into the kitchen.

"You have it bad, man," Paul said.

"Huh?" Abner turned his attention back to Paul.

"You're really smitten with her, aren't you?" Paul laughed. "I don't blame you. She's beautiful."

"She's more than that. She's loving, kind, thoughtful, generous, caring—"

Paul held up a hand to stop the flow of words. "I get it. I get it. She's the most wonderful girl in the world."

"*Jah*, she is," Abner agreed.

"So are you two gonna get married?"

Abner glanced around, but the people behind and in front of them were engrossed in conversation, so they hadn't overhead Paul's question. "Now that we're with the church, I can ask her, but"—he concentrated on the wide wooden floorboards under his feet—"I won't do that until I can afford to support her."

Unfortunately, that might be years from now. Myron had convinced the new shop owners to hire Abner, but most of his small salary went to supporting *Mamm* and his brothers. He'd been searching for another job, but so far, he'd had no luck.

Now that he'd joined the church, he could court Rebecca, but he wouldn't ask her to marry him. Not until he could afford it.

After everyone had finished eating, Abner helped various members of the congregation hook up their horses, while Paul stood off to the side, observing. Jakob was one of the last to get his buggy.

"Rebecca's finally finished helping your *mamm* in the kitchen," Jakob said with a smile.

"*Mamm* really appreciated her assistance all week. Although she's much healthier, she still tires easily, so we're both grateful to Rebecca."

Paul strode over. "I'd really like to talk to her and Abner before you leave."

Jakob frowned. "I don't think—"

"It won't take long," Paul assured him. "You can stand and watch us to be sure everything's above board."

Rebecca emerged from the house, and Paul waved her over. Jakob's brow furrowed even more as she crossed the lawn and headed toward them.

"Don't take too long," Jakob warned her.

Rebecca nodded and then followed as Paul beckoned her a short distance away from the men and boys who were hitching their horses.

"First of all," Paul said, "I'm so happy I could be here for your baptism. Thank you for inviting me. The reason I came, though, is to talk to you about this." He pulled a thick envelope from his pocket addressed to Abner. Herman's name and the studio address had been embossed in the upper left corner.

Abner tensed. Paul had assured him giving up his salary had covered all the costs of the apartment, transportation, and food. But Herman had threatened to sue for breach of contract and the extra production costs of hiring a new trainer. If Abner owed them that money, he couldn't ask Rebecca to wait for years.

Reluctantly, he took the envelope Paul held out. He opened it clumsily, and one of the papers inside fluttered to the ground. He bent to retrieve it but froze. "What's this?"

"Your pay for working on the show."

Abner picked up the check. "I can't accept this. We agreed my salary would cover the costs of renting the apartment."

"I know," Paul said, "but the pilot's been such a huge success. Herman's feeling generous. He decided the work you did was worth this amount as well as the cost of the apartment. The paperwork in the envelope has been notarized, so he can't go back on his word."

"But—but…" Abner stammered. With this much money, he could cover the mortgage on the farm and build a small place for himself and Rebecca.

Paul took the envelope from his nerveless fingers and pulled out a sheaf of papers. "You can read through all of this later, but I wanted you and Rebecca to see this." He motioned for her to come closer.

Abner could hardly breathe as Rebecca stood so close their arms brushed. His eyes blurred as he scanned the paragraph Paul pointed out.

As of this date, Abner Lapp's screen test and all subsequent copies have been destroyed.

"All of them are gone?" Rebecca's breathless whisper made Abner long to pull her into his arms.

Paul grinned. "That's right. I went through all the files to be sure every last one was deleted. You're now free and clear."

"Thank you, Paul," she said, and Abner echoed her words. Then her eyes misty, Rebecca gazed up at him. "Oh, Abner."

Abner clutched his suspenders to keep from wrapping his arms around her.

She flashed him the gorgeous smile that made his heart race and set his world on fire. The smile that made him want to do anything for her. And now he could. And this time her smile also held a promise for their future.

Rebecca floated home, barely hearing her family's conversation around her. The cloud hanging over her and Abner had been lifted. Never again would they fear having their reputations destroyed by that film. She'd learned a valuable lesson, and so had Abner. God had blessed them beyond belief today, and her heart was humming a jubilant melody.

Speaking of melodies, Abner would be picking her up for the singing soon. She could hardly wait.

When he arrived in his courting buggy, he helped her in and tucked a quilt around her. Although the fall air was nippy, Rebecca had no need for a cover because being near Abner heated her from head to toe. After he climbed into the driver's seat, he picked up the reins with one hand and slid the other under the blanket to entwine his fingers with hers.

"I read the letter and signed agreement from Herman. Everything Paul said earlier is true, and the contract also added another section he hadn't mentioned."

Rebecca flinched. She prayed it wouldn't be bad news or take away any of the other promises. "What did it say?"

"I didn't really understand it all. The wording confused me, but Paul explained it. Herman decided—maybe with some arm twisting from Paul—to pay me royalties from the show. He said I'd sparked the idea that led to his successful show."

"Royalties?"

"Herman will pay me a tiny portion of the money the show generates. I told Paul I didn't want to be paid, but he insisted it's too late to change a notarized document. He said they drew it up that way because he figured now that I've joined the church, I wouldn't sign a contract." Abner's face reddened.

Rebecca squeezed his hand. No doubt he was remembering when he almost signed that contract to act in the TV show. Hard to believe that was less than a year ago. So much had happened since then. And they'd both turned their lives around.

After they arrived at his house and he'd unhitched the horse, Abner took her hand as they crossed the backyard and went inside. Adah smiled as she spied them holding hands.

"Can I help you with anything?" Rebecca asked her.

"Could you slice some of these pies while Abner and Peter get the tables ready for tonight?" Adah waved toward several snitz pies on the counter.

Abner's look of reluctance as he left the room made Rebecca's heart swell. Every look, every gesture spoke of his love and caring. God had blessed her with the most wonderful man.

After she'd arranged pie slices on platters and set them out on the serving table, Rebecca turned to Adah. "What else can I do?"

Adah patted her shoulder. "You can take good care of my son."

That was one promise Rebecca would gladly make.

* * *

Abner could stay in the kitchen and gaze at Rebecca all evening, but he forced himself to get to work. He enjoyed brief glimpses of her as she flitted in and out of the kitchen to set food on the serving table. And once everyone arrived, he sat directly across from her while they played games before the hymn sing. He could gaze at her to his heart's content and enjoy her clear, bell-like voice when she sang.

Despite his enjoyment, he couldn't wait for the evening to end. By the time it did, he was a bundle of nerves. Rebecca stood by his side to bid everyone goodbye, then with fingers laced together, they headed for his courting buggy. Peter had hitched up the horse, and Abner helped Rebecca in. Once again, he wrapped her in a blanket.

This time, though, he clutched the reins with both hands as he took the long way home. When they came to the spot he'd chosen on the deserted back road, he pulled onto a small patch of gravel surrounded by trees.

Rebecca turned toward him, and the blanket slipped down to her lap. Abner reached for both of her hands.

Moonlight made her eyes sparkle. He swallowed hard. All the words he'd rehearsed fled. She was so beautiful and so precious. Her rejection a year ago had devastated him. What if she said *no* again?

Taking a deep breath, he said, "I know our courtship began before it should, and you were right to break it off. Now that we've both joined the church, I hope we can start again."

"Of course." Rebecca's smile lit her face and set his heart ablaze.

"I love you," he said, his voice husky, "and I always will." He wrapped his arms around her and cradled her head against his chest. Waiting all these months had been unbearable, but now at last, they could be together.

"I love you too."

Her sweet reassurance gave him courage to ask the question burning in his heart and soul. "Would you do me the honor of being my wife?"

Her answering *yes* fanned the fire into a blaze. She tipped her head to gaze into his eyes. "We've waited so long," she said.

Abner couldn't wait another minute. He lowered his head and met her upturned lips. As the kiss deepened, the flames exploded into fireworks that lit the night sky around him. With the woman he loved in his arms and his new relationship with God, he had everything he'd always longed for and dreamed of.

Because of God's love and forgiveness, they could face life together clean, fresh, and forgiven. Their future together glittered as clear and bright as the stars twinkling overhead.

* * * * *

SPECIAL EXCERPT FROM

Love Inspired®

*Paralyzed veteran Eve Vincent is happy with the
life she's built for herself at Mercy Ranch—until her
ex-fiancé shows up with a baby. Their best friends died
and named Eve and Ethan Forester as guardians.
But can they put their differences aside and build a
future together?*

Read on for a sneak preview of
Her Oklahoma Rancher *by Brenda Minton,
available June 2019 from Love Inspired!*

"I'm sorry, Eve, but I had to do something to make you see how important this is. We can't just walk away from her. It might not be what we signed on for and I feel like I'm the last person who should be raising this little girl, but James and Hanna trusted us."

"But there is no *us*," she said with a lift of her chin, but he could see pain reflected in her dark eyes.

The pain he saw didn't bother him as much as what he didn't see in her eyes, in her expression. He didn't see the person he used to know, the woman he'd planned to marry.

He had noticed the same yesterday, and he guessed that was why he'd left Tori with her. He'd been sitting there looking at a woman he used to think he knew better than he knew himself, and he hadn't recognized her.

"There is no *us*, but we still exist, you and me, and Tori needs us." He said it softly because the little girl in his arms seemed to be drifting off, even with the occasional sob.

"There has to be another option. I obviously can't do this. Last night was proof."

"Last night meant nothing. You've always managed, Eve. You're strong and capable."

"Before, Ethan. I was that person before. This is me now, and I can't."

"I guess you have changed. I've never heard you say you can't do anything."

He sat down on a nearby chair. Isaac had left. The woman named Sierra had also disappeared. They were alone. When had they last been alone? The night he proposed? It had been the night she left for Afghanistan. He'd taken her to dinner in San Antonio and they'd walked along the riverfront surrounded by people, music and twinkling lights.

He'd dropped to one knee there in front of strangers passing by, seeing the sights. Dozens had stopped to watch as she cried and said yes. Later they'd made the drive to the airport, his ring glistening on her finger, planning a wedding that would never happen.

"Ethan?" Her voice was soft, quiet, questioning.

He glanced down at the little girl in his arms.

"What other option is there, Eve? Should we turn her over to the state, let her take her chances with whoever they choose? Should we find some distant relative? What do you recommend?"

He leaned back in the chair and studied her face, her expression. She was everything familiar. His childhood friend. The person he'd loved. *Had* loved. Past tense. The woman he'd wanted to spend his life with had been someone else, someone who never backed down. She looked as tough, as stubborn as ever, but there was something fragile in her expression.

Something in her expression made him recheck his feelings. He'd been bucked off horses, trampled by a bull, broken his arm jumping dirt bikes. She'd been his only broken heart. He didn't want another one.

Don't miss
Her Oklahoma Rancher *by Brenda Minton,*
available June 2019 wherever
Love Inspired® books and ebooks are sold.

www.LoveInspired.com

LIEXP0619

Looking for inspiration in tales
of hope, faith and heartfelt romance?

Check out **Love Inspired**® and
Love Inspired® **Suspense** books!

New books available every month!

CONNECT WITH US AT:

Facebook.com/groups/HarlequinConnection

Facebook.com/HarlequinBooks

Twitter.com/HarlequinBooks

Instagram.com/HarlequinBooks

Pinterest.com/HarlequinBooks

ReaderService.com

Love Inspired®

WE HOPE YOU
ENJOYED THIS

LOVE
INSPIRED®
SUSPENSE
BOOK.

Discover more **heart-pounding** romances of **danger** and **faith** from the Love Inspired Suspense series.

Be sure to look for all six Love Inspired Suspense books every month.

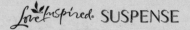 *Love Inspired®* SUSPENSE

www.LoveInspired.com

K-9 officer Gavin Sutherland held tight to his K-9 partner Tommy's leash and scanned the crowd, his mind on high alert, his whole body tense as he tried to protect the city he loved. People from all over the world stood shoulder to shoulder along the East River, waiting for the annual Fourth of July fireworks display.

His partner, a black-and-white springer spaniel, knew the drill. Tommy worked bomb detection. He had been trained to find incendiary devices. He knew to sniff the air and the ground. Sniff, sit, repeat. Be rewarded.

Glancing up, Gavin spotted his backup, K-9 officer Brianne Hayes, a rookie who had been paired with him to continue gaining experience.

Brianne headed toward him, her auburn hair caught up in a severe bun. That fire-colored hair matched her fierce determination to prove herself since she was one of only a few female K-9 officers in the city that never slept.

LISEXP0619

Brianne's partner, Stella, was also in training with the K-9 handlers.

"I've been along the perimeters of the park," Brianne said. "Nothing out of the ordinary. Can't wait for the show."

Scanning the area again, he said, "I think the crowd grows every year. Standing room only tonight."

"Stella keeps fidgeting and sniffing. She needs to get used to this."

Stella stopped and lifted her nose into the air, a soft growl emitting from her throat.

"Steady, girl. You'll need to contain that when the fireworks start."

But Stella didn't quit. The big dog tugged forward, her nose sniffing both air and ground.

Gavin watched the Labrador, wondering what kind of scent she'd picked up. Then Tommy alerted, going still except for his wagging tail that acted like a warning flag, his body trembling in place.

"Something's up," Gavin whispered to Brianne. "He's picked up a signature somewhere."

Brianne whispered low. "There's a bomb?"

Don't miss
Deep Undercover *by Lenora Worth,*
available July 2019 wherever
Love Inspired® Suspense books and ebooks are sold.

www.LoveInspired.com

Inspirational Romance to Warm Your Heart and Soul

Join our social communities to connect with other readers who share your love!

Sign up for the Love Inspired newsletter at **www.LoveInspired.com** to be the first to find out about upcoming titles, special promotions and exclusive content.

CONNECT WITH US AT:

Facebook.com/groups/HarlequinConnection

 Facebook.com/LoveInspiredBooks

 Twitter.com/LoveInspiredBks

LISOCIAL2018